THE TWILIGHT OF THE SIOUX

Books by John G. Neihardt
published by the University of Nebraska Press

THE
TWILIGHT
OF THE
SIOUX

The Song of the Indian Wars
The Song of the Messiah

Volume II of *A Cycle of the West*

BY

JOHN G. NEIHARDT

UNIVERSITY OF NEBRASKA • LINCOLN/LONDON

∞

INTRODUCTION

In 1912, at the age of 31, I began work on the following cycle of heroic *Songs*, designed to celebrate the great mood of courage that was developed west of the Missouri River in the nineteenth century. The series was dreamed out, much of it in detail, before I began; and for years it was my hope that it might be completed at the age of 60—as it was. During the interval, more than five thousand days were devoted to the work, along with the fundamentally important business of being first a man and a father. It was planned from the beginning that the five *Songs*, which appeared at long intervals during a period of twenty-nine years, should constitute a single work. They are now offered as such.

The period with which the *Cycle* deals was one of discovery, exploration and settlement—a genuine epic period, differing in no essential from the other great epic periods that marked the advance of the Indo-European peoples out of Asia and across Europe. It was a time of intense individualism, a time when society was cut loose from its

[v]

roots, a time when an old culture was being overcome by that of a powerful people driven by the ancient needs and greeds. For this reason only, the word "epic" has been used in connection with the *Cycle*; it is properly descriptive of the mood and meaning of the time and of the material with which I have worked. There has been no thought of synthetic *Iliads* and *Odysseys,* but only of the richly human saga-stuff of a country that I knew and loved, and of a time in the very fringe of which I was a boy.

This period began in 1822 and ended in 1890. The dates are not arbitrary. In 1822 General Ashley and Major Henry led a band of a hundred trappers from St. Louis, "the Mother of the West," to the beaver country of the upper Missouri River. During the following year a hundred more Ashley-Henry men ascended the Missouri. Out of these trapper bands came all the great continental explorers after Lewis and Clark. It was they who discovered and explored the great central route by way of South Pass, from the Missouri River to the Pacific Ocean, over which the tide of migration swept westward from the 40's onward.

The Song of Three Friends and *The Song of Hugh Glass* deal with the ascent of the river and with characteristic adventures of Ashley-Henry men in the country of the upper Missouri and the Yellowstone.

The Song of Jed Smith follows the first band of Americans through South Pass to the Great Salt Lake, the first band of Americans to reach Spanish California by an overland trail, the first white men to cross the great central desert from the Sierras to Salt Lake.

The Song of the Indian Wars deals with the period of migration and the last great fight for the bison pastures between the invading white race and the Plains Indians—the Sioux, the Cheyenne and the Arapahoe.

The Song of the Messiah is concerned wholly with the conquered people and the worldly end of their last great dream. The period closes with the Battle of Wounded Knee in 1890, which marked the end of Indian resistance on the Plains.

It will have been noted from the foregoing that the five *Songs* are linked in chronological order; but in addition to their progress in time and across the vast land, those who may feel as I have felt while the tales were growing may note a spiritual progression also—from the level of indomitable physical prowess to that of spiritual triumph in apparent worldly defeat. If any vital question be suggested in *The Song of Jed Smith*, for instance, there may be those who will find its age-old answer once again in the final *Song* of an alien people who also were men, and troubled.

But, after all, "the play's the thing"; and while

it is true that a knowledge of Western history and the topography of the country would be very helpful to a reader of the *Cycle*, such knowledge is not indispensable. For here are tales of men in struggle, triumph and defeat.

Those readers who have not followed the development of the *Cycle* may wish to know, and are entitled to know, something of my fitness for the task assumed a generation ago and now completed. To those I may say that I did not experience the necessity of seeking material about which to write. The feel and mood of it were in the blood of my family, and my early experiences aroused a passionate awareness of it. My family came to Pennsylvania more than a generation before the Revolutionary War, in which fourteen of us fought; and, crossing the Alleghenies after the war, we did not cease pioneering until some of us reached Oregon. Any one of my heroes, from point of time, could have been my paternal grandfather, who was born in 1801.

My maternal grandparents were covered-wagon people, and at the age of five I was living with them in a sod house on the upper Solomon in western Kansas. The buffalo had vanished from that country only a few years before, and the signs of them were everywhere. I have helped, as a little boy could, in "picking cow-chips" for winter fuel. If I write of hot-winds and grasshoppers, of prairie fires and blizzards, of dawns and noons and sunsets and nights, of brooding heat and thunderstorms in vast lands, I knew them early. They were the vital facts of my world, along with the talk of the old-timers who knew such fascinating things to talk about.

I was a very little boy when my father introduced me to the Missouri River at Kansas City. It was flood time. The impression was tremendous, and a steadily growing desire to know what had happened on such a river led me directly to my heroes. Twenty years later, when I had come to know them well, I built a boat at Fort Benton, Montana, descended the Missouri in low water and against head winds, dreamed back the stories men had lived along the river, bend by bend. This experience is set forth in *The River and I*.

In northern Nebraska I grew up at the edge of the retreating frontier, and became intimately associated with the Omaha Indians, a Siouan people, when many of the old "long-hairs" among them still remembered vividly the time that meant so much to me. We were good friends. Later, I became equally well acquainted among the Oglala Sioux, as my volume, *Black Elk Speaks*, reveals; and I have never been happier than while living with my friends among them, mostly unreconstructed "long-hairs," sharing, as one of them, their thoughts, their feelings, their rich memories that often reached far back into the world of my *Cycle*.

When I have described battles, I have depended far less on written accounts than upon the reminiscences of men who fought in them—not only Indians, but whites as well. For, through many years, I was privileged to know many old white men, officers and privates, who had fought in the Plains Wars. Much of the material for the last two *Songs* of the series came directly from those who were themselves a part of the stories.

For the first three *Songs*, I was compelled to depend chiefly upon early journals of travel and upon an intimate knowledge of Western history generally. But while I could not have known my earlier heroes, I have known old men who had missed them, but had known men who knew some of them well; and such memories at second hand can be most illuminating to one who knows the facts already. For instance, I once almost touched even Jedediah Smith himself, the greatest and most mysterious of them all, through an old plainsman who was an intimate friend of Bridger, who had been a comrade of Jed!

Such intimate contacts with soldiers, plainsmen, Indians and river men were an integral part of my life for many years, and I cannot catalog them here. As for knowledge of the wide land with which the *Cycle* deals, those who know any part of it well will know that I have been there too.

Those who are not acquainted with early Western history will find a good introduction to the *Cycle* in Harrison Dale's *The Ashley-Henry Men* —or perhaps my own book, *The Splendid Wayfaring*.

I can see now that I grew up on the farther slope of a veritable "watershed of history," the summit of which is already crossed, and in a land where the old world lingered longest. It is gone, and, with it, all but two or three of the old-timers, white and brown, whom I have known. My mind and most of my heart are with the young, and with the strange new world that is being born in agony. But something of my heart stays yonder, for in the years of my singing about a time and a country that I loved, I note, without regret, that I have become an old-timer myself!

The foregoing was set down in anticipation of some questions that readers of good will, potential friends, might ask.

JOHN NEIHARDT

Columbia, Mo., 1948.

THE SONG OF THE INDIAN WARS

TO ALICE, THREE YEARS OLD

When I began the gift I bear
It seemed you weren't anywhere;
But being younger now I know
How even fifty moons ago
The apple bloom began to seek
The proper tinting for a cheek;
The skies, aware of thrilling news,
Displayed the loveliest of blues
For whoso fashions eyes to choose.
And all that prehistoric spring
Experimental grace of wing
And tentatively shapen forms,
From crocuses to thunderstorms,
And happy sound and sunny glow
Rehearsed you fifty moons ago.
Why, even I was toiling too
Upon a little gift for you!
And now that we are wise and three,
And I love you and you love me,
We know the whole conspiracy!

I. THE SOWING OF THE DRAGON

At last the four year storm of fratricide
Had ceased at Appomattox, and the tide
Of war-bit myriads, like a turning sea's,
Recoiled upon the deep realities
That yield no foam to any squall of change.

Now many a hearth of home had gotten
    strange
To eyes that knew sky-painting flares of war.
So much that once repaid the striving for
No longer mattered. Yonder road that ran
At hazard once beyond the ways of Man
By haunted vale and space-enchanted hill,
Had never dreamed of aught but Jones's
    Mill—
A dull pedestrian! The spring, where erst
The peering plowboy sensed a larger thirst,
Had shoaled from awe, so long the man had
    drunk
At deeper floods. How yonder field had
    shrunk
That billowed once mysteriously far
To where the cow-lot nursed the evening
    star
And neighbored with the drowsing moon and
    sun!
For O what winds of wrath had boomed and
    run

Across what vaster fields of moaning grain—
Rich seedings, nurtured by a ghastly rain
To woeful harvest!

                    So the world went small.
But 'mid the wreck of things remembered tall
An epidemic rumor murmured now.
Men leaned upon the handles of the plow
To hear and dream; and through the harrow-
          smoke
The weird voice muttered and the vision broke
Of distant, princely acres unpossessed.

Again the bugles of the Race blew west
That once the Tigris and Euphrates heard.
In unsuspected deeps of being stirred
The ancient and compelling Aryan urge.
A homing of the homeless, surge on surge,
The valley roads ran wagons, and the hills
Through lane and by-way fed with trickling
          rills
The man-stream mighty with a mystic thaw.
All summer now the Mississippi saw
What long ago the Hellespont beheld.
The shrewd, prophetic eyes that peered of eld
Across the Danube, visioned naked plains
Beyond the bleak Missouri, clad with grains,
Jewelled with orchard, grove and greening
          garth—
Serene abundance centered in a hearth
To nurture lusty children.

                    On they swirled,
The driving breed, the takers of the world,

The makers and the bringers of the law.
Now up along the bottoms of the Kaw
The drifting reek of wheel and hoof arose.
The kiotes talked about it and the crows
Along the lone Republican; and still
The bison saw it on the Smoky Hill
And Solomon; while yonder on the Platte
Ten thousand wagons scarred the sandy flat
Between the green grass season and the brown.

A name sufficed to make the camp a town,
A whim unmade. In spaces wide as air,
And late as empty, now the virile share
Quickened the virgin meadow-lands of God;
And lo, begotten of the selfsame sod,
The house and harvest!

        So the Cadmian breed,
The wedders of the vision and the deed,
Went forth to sow the dragon-seed again.

But there were those—and they were also men—
Who saw the end of sacred things and dear
In all this wild beginning; saw with fear
Ancestral pastures gutted by the plow,
The bison harried ceaselessly, and how
They dwindled moon by moon; with pious
    dread
Beheld the holy places of their dead
The mock of aliens.

        Sioux, Arapahoe,
Cheyenne, Commanche, Kiowa and Crow
In many a council pondered what befell
The prairie world. Along the Musselshell,

The Tongue, the Niobrara, all they said
Upon the Platte, the Arkansaw, the Red
Was echoed word by peril-laden word.
Along Popo Agie [1] and the Horn they heard
The clank of hammers and the clang of rails
Where hordes of white men conjured iron trails
Now crawling past the Loup Fork and the
    Blue.
By desert-roaming Cimarron they knew,
And where La Poudre heads the tale was
    known,
How, snoring up beyond the Yellowstone,
The medicine-canoes breathed flame and steam
And, like weird monsters of an evil dream,
Spewed foes—a multitudinary spawn!

Were all the teeming regions of the dawn
Unpeopled now? What devastating need
Had set so many faces pale with greed
Against the sunset? Not as men who seek
Some meed of kindness, suppliant and meek,
These hungry myriads came. They did but
    look,
And whatsoever pleased them, that they took.
Their faded eyes were icy, lacking ruth,
And all their tongues were forked to split the
    truth
That word and deed might take diverging ways.
Bewildered in the dusk of ancient days
The Red Men groped; and howsoever loud
The hopeful hotheads boasted in the crowd,
The wise ones heard prophetic whisperings
Through aching hushes; felt the end of things

[1] Pronounced *Po-po-zha.*

[4]

Inexorably shaping.   What should be
Already was to them.   And who can flee
His shadow or his doom?   Though cowards
    stride
The wind-wild thunder-horses, Doom shall ride
The arrows of the lightning, and prevail.
Ere long whole tribes must take the spirit trail
As once they travelled to the bison hunt.
Then let it be with many wounds—in front—
And many scalps, to show their ghostly kin
How well they fought the fight they could not
    win,
To perish facing what they could not kill.

So down upon the Platte and Smoky Hill
Swept war; and all their valleys were afraid.
The workers where the trails were being laid
To speed the iron horses, now must get
Their daily wage in blood as well as sweat
With gun and shovel.   Often staring plains
Beheld at daybreak gutted wagon-trains
Set foursquare to the whirling night-attack,
With neither hoof nor hand to bring them back
To Omaha or Westport.   Every week
The rolling coaches bound for Cherry Creek
Were scarred in running battle.   Every day
Some ox-rig, creeping California way—
That paradise of every hope fulfilled—
Was plundered and the homesick driver killed,
Forlornly fighting for his little brood.
And often was the prairie solitude
Aware by night of burning ricks and roofs,
Stampeding cattle and the fleeing hoofs
Of wild marauders.

II. RED CLOUD

                      Sullenly a gale
That blustered rainless up the Bozeman Trail
Was bringing June again; but not the dear
Deep-bosomed mother of a hemisphere
That other regions cherish. Flat of breast,
More passionate than loving, up the West
A stern June strode, lean suckler of the lean,
Her rag-and-tatter robe of faded green
Blown dustily about her.

                      Afternoon
Now held the dazzled prairie in a swoon;
And where the Platte and Laramie unite,
The naked heavens slanted blinding light
Across the bare Fort Laramie parade.
The groping shadow-arm the flag-pole swayed
To nightward, served to emphasize the
     glare;
And 'mid Saharan hollows of the air
One haughty flower budded from the mast
And bloomed and withered as the gale soughed
     past
To languish in the swelter.

                     Growing loud,
When some objection wakened in the crowd,

Or dwindling to a murmur of assent,
Still on and on the stubborn parley went
Of many treaty makers gathered here.
Big talk there was at Laramie that year
Of 'sixty-six; for lo, a mighty word
The Great White Father spoke, and it was
        heard
From peep of morning to the sunset fires.
The southwind took it from the talking wires
And gave it to the gusty west that blew
Its meaning down the country of the Sioux
Past Inyan Kara to Missouri's tide.
The eager eastwind took and flung it wide
To where lush valleys gaze at lofty snow
All summer long. And now Arapahoe
The word was; now Dakota; now Cheyenne;
But still one word: 'Let grass be green again
Upon the trails of war and hatred cease,
For many presents and the pipe of peace
Are waiting yonder at the Soldier's Town!'
And there were some who heard it with a
        frown
And said, remembering the White Man's guile:
"Make yet more arrows when the foemen
        smile."
And others, wise with many winters, said:
"Life narrows, and the better days are dead.
Make war upon the sunset! Will it stay?"
And some who counselled with a dream would
        say:
"Great Spirit made all peoples, White and Red,
And pitched one big blue teepee overhead
That men might live as brothers side by side.
Behold! Is not our country very wide,

With room enough for all?"   And there were some
Who answered scornfully: "Not so they come;
Their medicine is strong, their hearts are bad;
A little part of what our fathers had
They give us now, tomorrow come and take.
Great Spirit also made the rattlesnake
And over him the big blue teepee set!"

So wrought the Great White Father's word; and yet,
Despite remembered and suspected wrong,
Because the Long Knife's medicine was strong,
There lacked not mighty chieftains who obeyed.
A thousand Ogalalas Man Afraid
And Red Cloud marshalled on the council trail;
A thousand Brulés followed Spotted Tail.
Cheyennes, Arapahoes came riding down
By hundreds; till the little Soldier Town
Was big with teepees.

Where the white June drowse
Beat slanting through a bower of withered boughs
That cast a fretwork travesty of shade,
Now sat the peace-commissioners and made
Soft words to woo the chieftains of the bands.
'They wanted but a roadway through the lands
Wherein the Rosebud, Tongue and Powder head,
That white men, seeking for the yellow lead
Along the Madison, might pass that way.
There ran the shortest trail by many a day

Of weary travel.   This could do no harm;
Nor would there be occasion for alarm
If they should wish to set a fort or two
Up yonder—not against Cheyenne and Sioux,
But rather that the Great White Father's will
Might be a curb upon his people still
And Red Men's rights be guarded by the laws.'

Adroitly phrased, with many a studied pause,
In which the half-breed spokesmen, bit by bit,
Reshaped the alien speech and scattered it,
The purpose of the council swept at last
Across the lounging crowd.   And where it passed
The feathered headgear swayed and bent
        together
With muttering, as when in droughty weather
A little whirlwind sweeps the tasseled corn.
Some bull-lunged Ogalala's howl of scorn
Was hurled against the few assenting "hows"
Among the Brulés.   Then the summer drowse
Came back, the vibrant silence of the heat;
For Man Afraid had gotten to his feet,
His face set hard, one straight arm rising slow
Against the Whites, as though he bent a bow
And yonder should the fleshing arrow fly.
So stood he, and the moments creeping by
Were big with expectation.   Still and tense,
The council felt the wordless eloquence
Of Man Afraid; and then:

                              "I tell you no!
When Harney talked to us ten snows ago
He gave us all that country.   Now you say
The White Chief lied.   My heart is bad today,

Because I know too well the forkéd tongue
That makes a promise when the moon is young,
And kills it when the moon is in the dark!"

The Ogalalas roared; and like a spark
That crawls belated when the fuse is damp,
The words woke sequent thunders through
    the camp
Where Cheyennes heard it and Arapahoes.
Then once again the chieftain's voice arose:
"Your talk is sweet today. So ever speak
The white men when they know their hands
    are weak
That itch to steal. But once your soldiers pitch
Their tepees yonder, will the same hands itch
The less for being stronger? Go around.
I do not want you in my hunting ground!
You scare my bison, and my folk must eat.
Far sweeter than your words are, home is sweet
To us, as you; and yonder land is home.
In sheltered valleys elk and bison roam
All winter there, and in the spring are fat.
We gave the road you wanted up the Platte.
Make dust upon it then! But you have said
The shortest way to find the yellow lead
Runs yonder. Any trail is short enough
That leads your greedy people to the stuff
That makes them crazy! It is bad for you.
I, Man Afraid, have spoken. *Hetchetu!*"

How, how, how, how! A howl of fighting men
Swept out across the crowd and back again
To break about the shadow-mottled stand
Where Colonel Maynadier, with lifted hand,

Awaited silence. 'As a soldier should,
He spoke straight words and few. His heart
        was good.
The Great White Father would be very sad
To know the heart of Man Afraid was bad
And how his word was called a crooked word.
It could not be that Man Afraid had heard.
The council had not said that Harney lied.
It wanted but a little road, as wide
As that a wagon makes from wheel to wheel.
The Long Knife chieftains had not come to steal
The Red Men's hunting ground.'

                        The half-breeds cried
The speech abroad; but where it fell, it died.
One heard the flag a-ripple at the mast,
The bicker of the river flowing past,
The melancholy crooning of the gale.

Now 'mid the bodeful silence, Spotted Tail
Arose, and all the people leaned to hear;
For was he not a warrior and a seer
Whose deeds were mighty as his words were
        wise?
Some droll, shrewd spirit in his narrowed eyes
Seemed peering past the moment and afar
To where predestined things already are;
And humor lurked beneath the sober mien,
But half concealed, as though the doom fore-
        seen
Revealed the old futility of tears.
Remembering the story of his years,
His Brulé warriors loved him standing so.
And some recalled that battle long ago

Far off beside the upper Arkansaw,
When, like the freshet of a sudden thaw,
The Utes came down; and how the Brulés, caught
In ambush, sang the death-song as they fought,
For many were the foes and few were they;
Yet Spotted Tail, a stripling fresh from play,
Had saved them with his daring and his wit.
How often when the dark of dawn was lit
With flaming wagon-tops, his battle-cry
Had made it somehow beautiful to die,
A whirlwind joy! And how the leaping glare
Had shown by fits the snow-fall of despair
Upon the white men's faces! Well they knew
That every brave who followed him was two,
So mighty was the magic of his name.
And none forgot the first time Harney came—
His whetted deaths that chattered in the sheath,
The long blue snake that set the ground beneath
A-smoulder with a many-footed rage.
What bleeding of the Brulés might assuage
That famished fury? Vain were cunning words
To pay the big arrears for harried herds
And desolated homes and settlers slain
And many a looted coach and wagon-train
And all that sweat of terror in the land!
Who now went forth to perish, that his band
Might still go free? Lo, yonder now he stood!
And none forgot his loving hardihood
The day he put the ghost paint on his face
And, dressed for death, went singing to the place
Where Harney's soldiers waited.

                    "Brothers, friends!"
Slow words he spoke. "The longest summer ends,
And nothing stays forever. We are old.
Can anger check the coming of the cold?
When frosts begin men think of meat and wood
And how to make the days of winter good
With what the summer leaves them of its cheer.
Two times I saw the first snow deepen here,
The last snow melt; and twice the grass was
          brown
When I was living at the Soldier's Town
To save my Brulés. All the while I thought
About this alien people I had fought,
Until a cloud was lifted from my eyes.
I saw how some great spirit makes them wise.
I saw a white Missouri flowing men,
And knew old times could never be again
This side of where the spirit sheds its load.
Then let us give the Powder River road,
For they will take it if we do not give.
Not all can die in battle. Some must live.
I think of those and what is best for those.
Dakotas, I have spoken."

                              Cries arose
From where his band of Brulé warriors sat—
The cries that once sent Panic up the Platte,
An eyeless runner panting through the gloom.
For though their chief had seen the creeping
          doom
Like some black cloud that gnaws the prairie
          rim,
Yet echoes of their charges under him
Had soared and sung above the words he said.
                    [13]

Now silence, like some music of the dead
That holds a throng of new-born spirits awed,
Possessed the brooding crowd. A lone crow
    cawed.
A wind fled moaning like a wildered ghost.

So clung that vatic hush upon the host
Until the Bad Face Ogalala band
Saw Red Cloud coming forward on the stand,
Serene with conscious might, a king of men.
Then all the hills were ululant again
As though a horde of foes came charging there;
For here was one who never gave despair
A moral mien, nor schooled a righteous hate
To live at peace with evil. Tall and straight
He stood and scanned the now quiescent
    crowd;
Then faced the white commissioners and
    bowed
A gracious bow—the gesture of a knight
Whose courage pays due deference to might
Before the trumpets breathe the battle's
    breath.
Not now he seemed that fearful lord of death,
Whose swarm of charging warriors, clad in red,
Were like a desolating thunder-head
Against an angry sunset. Many a Sioux
Recalled the time he fought alone and slew
His father's slayers, Bull Bear and his son,
While yet a fameless youth; and many a one
About the fort, remembering Grattán
And all his troopers slaughtered by a man
So bland of look and manner, wondered much.
Soft to the ear as velvet to the touch,

His speech, that lacked but little to be song,
Caressed the fringing hushes of the throng
Where many another's cry would scarce be
    clear.

"My brothers, when you see this prairie here,
You see my mother. Forty snows and four
Have blown and melted since the son she bore
First cried at Platte Forks yonder, weak and
    blind;
And whether winter-stern or summer-kind,
Her ways with me were wise. Her thousand
    laps
Have shielded me. Her ever-giving paps
Have suckled me and made me tall for war.
What presents shall I trade my mother for?
A string of beads? A scarlet rag or two?"

Already he was going ere they knew
That he had ceased. Among the people fled
A sound as when the frosted oaks are red
And naked thickets shiver in the flaws.
Far out among the lodges keened the squaws,
Shrill with a sorrow women understand,
As though the mother-passion of the land
Had found a human voice to claim the child.

With lifted brows the bland commission
    smiled,
As clever men who share a secret joke.

At length the Brulé, Swift Bear, rose and spoke,
'Twixt fear and favor poised. He seemed a man
Who, doubting both his ponies, rode the span

And used the quirt with caution. Black
    Horse then
Harangued the crowd a space, the words,
    Cheyenne,
Their sense, an echo of the White Man's plea,
Rebounding from a tense expectancy
Of many pleasing gifts.

                  But all the while
These wrestled with the question, mile on mile
The White Man's answer crept along the
    road—
Two hundred mule-teams, leaning to the load,
And seven hundred soldiers! Middle May
Had seen their dust cloud slowly trail away
From Kearney. Rising ever with the sun
And falling when the evening had begun,
It drifted westward. When the low-swung
    moon
Was like a cradle for the baby June,
They camped at Julesburg. Yet another
    week
Across the South Platte's flood to Pumpkin
    Creek
They fought the stubborn road. Beneath the
    towers
Of Court House Rock, awash in starry showers,
Their fagged herd grazed. Past Chimney Rock
    they crawled;
Past where the roadway narrows, dizzy walled;
Past Mitchell Post. And now, intent to win
Ere dusk to where the Laramie comes in,
The surly teamsters swore and plied the goad.
The lurching wagons grumbled at the road,

The trace-chains clattered and the spent mules
    brayed,
Protesting as the cracking lashes played
On lathered withers bitten to the red;
And, glinting in the slant glare overhead,
A big dust beckoned to the Soldier's Town.

It happened now that Red Cloud, peering down
The dazzling valley road with narrowed eyes,
Beheld that picture-writing on the skies
And knitted puzzled brows to make it out.
So, weighing this and that, a lonely scout
Might read a trail by moonlight. Loudly still
The glib logicians wrangled, as they will,
The freer for the prime essential lacked—
A due allowance for the Brutal Fact,
That, by the vulgar trick of being so,
Confounds logicians.

                            Lapsing in a flow
Of speech and counter-speech, a half hour
    passed
While Red Cloud stared and pondered. Then
    at last
Men saw him rise and leave his brooding place,
The flinty look of battle on his face,
A gripping claw of wrath between his brows.
Electric in the sullen summer drowse,
The silence deepened, waiting for his word;
But still he gazed, nor spoke. The people heard
The river lipping at a stony brink,
The rippling flag, then suddenly the clink
Of bridle-bits, the tinkling sound of spurs.
The chieftains and the white commissioners

Pressed forward with a buzzing of surprise.
The people turned.

                  Atop a gentle rise
That cut the way from fort to ford in half,
Came Carrington a-canter with his staff,
And yonder, miles behind, the reeking air
Revealed how many others followed there
To do his will.

               Now rising to a shout,
The voice of Red Cloud towered, crushing out
The wonder-hum that ran from band to band:
"These white men here have begged our
      hunting land.
Their words are crookéd and their tongues are
      split;
For even while they feign to beg for it,
Their soldiers come to steal it! Let them try,
And prove how good a warrior is a lie,
And learn how Ogalalas meet a thief!
You, Spotted Tail, may be the beggar's chief—
I go to keep my mother-land from harm!"
He tapped his rifle nestled in his arm.
"From now I put my trust in this!" he said
With lowered voice; then pointing overhead,
"Great Spirit, too, will help me!"

                    With a bound
He cleared the bower-railing for the ground,
And shouting "Bring the horses in," he made
His way across the turbulent parade
To where the Ogalala lodges stood.
So, driving down some hollow in a wood,

A great wind shoulders through the tangled
    ruck
And after it, swirled inward to the suck,
The crested timber roars.

                        Then, like a bird
That fills a sudden lull, again was heard
The clink of steel as Carrington rode through
The man-walled lane that cleft the crowd in
    two;
And, hobbling after, mindless of the awe
That favors might, a toothless, ancient squaw
Lifted a feeble fist at him and screamed.

III. THE COUNCIL ON THE POWDER

Serenely now the ghost of summer dreamed
On Powder River. 'Twas the brooding time,
With nights of starlight glinting on the rime
That cured the curly grass for winter feed,
And days of blue and gold when scarce a
    reed
Might stir along the runnels, lean with
    drouth.
Some few belated cranes were going south,
And any hour the blizzard wind might
    bawl;
But still the tawny fingers of the Fall,
Lay whist upon the maw of Winter.

                            Thrice
The moon had been a melting boat of ice
Among the burning breakers of the west,
Since Red Cloud, bitter-hearted, topped the
    crest
Above the Fort and took the homeward
    track,
The Bad Face Ogalalas at his back
And some few Brulés. Silently he rode,
And they who saw him bent as with a load
Of all the tribal sorrow that should be,
Pursued the trail as silently as he—
A fateful silence, boding little good.
Beyond the mouth of Bitter Cottonwood

They travelled; onward through the winding
    halls
Where Platte is darkened; and the listening
    walls
Heard naught of laughter—heard the ponies
    blow,
The rawhide creak upon the bent travaux,
The lodge-poles skid and slidder in the sand.
Nor yet beyond amid the meadowland
Was any joy; nor did the children play,
Despite the countless wooers by the way—
Wild larkspur, tulip, bindweed, prairie pea.
The shadow of a thing that was to be
Fell on them too, though what they could not
    tell.

Still on, beyond the Horseshoe and La Prele,
They toiled up Sage Creek where the prickly
    pear
Bloomed gaudily about the camp. And there
The Cheyenne, Black Horse, riding from the
    south,
Came dashing up with sugar in his mouth
To spew on bitter moods. "Come back," he
    whined;
"Our good white brothers call you, being kind
And having many gifts to give to those
Who hear them." But the braves unstrung
    their bows
And beat him from the village, counting
    coup,
While angry squaws reviled the traitor too,
And youngsters dogged him, aping what he
    said.

Across the barren Cheyenne watershed
Their ponies panted, where the sage brush roots
Bit deep to live. They saw the Pumpkin Buttes
From Dry Fork. Then the Powder led them
    down
A day past Lodge Pole Creek.

                Here Red Cloud's town,
With water near and grass enough, now stood
Amid a valley strewn with scrubby wood;
And idling in the lazy autumn air
The lodge-smoke rose. The only idler there!
For all day long the braves applied their hate
To scraping dogwood switches smooth and
    straight
For battle-arrows; and the teeth that bit
The gnarly shaft, put venom into it
Against the day the snarling shaft should bite.
Unceasingly from morning until night
The squaws toiled that their fighting men
    might eat,
Nor be less brave because of freezing feet.
By hundreds they were stitching rawhide soles
To buckskin uppers. Many drying-poles
Creaked with the recent hunt; and bladders,
    packed
With suet, fruit and flesh, were being stacked
For hungers whetted by the driving snow.
Fresh robes were tanning in the autumn glow
For warriors camping fireless in the cold.
And noisily the mimic battles rolled
Among the little children, grim in play.

The village had been growing day by day
Since Red Cloud sent a pipe to plead his cause

Among the far-flung Tetons. Hunkpapas,
Unhurried by the fear of any foe,
Were making winter meat along Moreau
The day the summons came to gird their loins.
The Sans Arcs, roving where the Belle Fourche
    joins
The Big Cheyenne, had smoked the proffered
    pipe
When grapes were good and plums were
    getting ripe.
Amid the Niobrara meadowlands
And up the White, the scattered Brulé bands,
That scorned the talk at Laramie, had heard.
Among the Black Hills went the pipe and word
To find the Minneconjoux killing game
Where elk and deer were plentiful and tame
And clear creeks bellowed from the canyon
    beds.
Still westward where the double Cheyenne
    heads,
The hunting Ogalalas hearkened too.
So grew the little camp as lakelets do
When coulees grumble to a lowering sky.

Big names, already like a battle cry,
Were common in the town; and there were
    some
In which terrific thunders yet were dumb
But soon should echo fearsome and abhorred:
Crow King, Big Foot, the younger Hump, and
    Sword,
Black Leg and Black Shield, Touch-the-Cloud
    and Gall;
And that one fear would trumpet over all—

Young Crazy Horse; and Spotted Tail, the wise;
Red Cloud and Man Afraid, both battle-cries;
Rain-in-the-Face, yet dumb; and Sitting Bull.

'Twas council time, for now the moon was full;
The time when, ere the stars may claim the
    dark,
A goblin morning with the owl for lark
Steals in; and ere the flags of day are furled,
Pressed white against the window of the world
A scarred face stares astonished at the sun.
The moonset and the sunrise came as one;
But ere the daybreak lifted by a span
The frosty dusk, the tepee tops began
To burgeon, and a faery sapling grove
Stood tall, to bloom in sudden red and mauve
And gold against the horizontal light.
Still humped, remembering the nipping night,
The dogs prowled, sniffing, round the open flaps
Where women carved raw haunches in their
    laps
To feed the kettles for the council feast.
Amid the silence of the lifting east
The criers shouted now—old men and sage,
Using the last sad privilege of age
For brief pathetic triumphs over youth.
Neat saws and bits of hortatory truth
They proffered with the orders of the day.
And names that were as scarlet in the gray
Of pending ill they uttered like a song—
The names of those who, being wise or strong,
Should constitute the council. 'Round and
    'round,
The focal centers of a spreading sound,

The criers went. The folk began to fuse
In groups that seized the latest bit of news
And sputtered with the tongue of fool and
    seer.
A roaring hailed some chanted name held dear;
Or in a silence, no less eloquent,
Some other, tainted with suspicion, went
Among the people like a wind that blows
In solitary places.

                    Day arose
A spear-length high. The chattering became
A bated hum; for, conscious of their fame,
And clad in gorgeous ceremonial dress,
The Fathers of the Council cleft the press
In lanes that awe ran on before to clear;
And expectation closed the flowing rear
Sucked in to where the council bower stood.
Long since the busy squaws had fetched the
    wood
And lit the council fire, now smouldering.
The great men entered, formed a broken ring
To open eastward, lest the Light should find
No entrance, and the leaders of the blind
See darkly too. With reverential awe
The people, pressed about the bower, saw
The fathers sit, and every tongue was stilled.

Now Red Cloud took the sacred pipe and filled
The bowl with fragrant bark, and plucked a
    brand
To light it. Now with slowly lifted hand
He held it to the glowing sky, and spoke:
"Grandfather, I have filled a pipe to smoke,

And you shall smoke it first. In you we trust
To show good trails." He held it to the dust.
"Grandmother, I have filled a pipe for you,"
He said, "and you must keep us strong and
        true,
For you are so." Then offering the stem
To all four winds, he supplicated them
That they should blow good fortune. Then he
        smoked;
And all the Fathers after him invoked
The Mysteries that baffle Man's desire.

Some women fetched and set beside the fire
The steaming kettles, then with groundward
        gaze
Withdrew in haste. A man of ancient days,
Who searched a timeless dusk with rheumy
        stare
And saw the ghosts of things that struggle
        there
Before men struggle, now remembered Those
With might to help. Six bits of meat he chose,
The best the pots afforded him, and these
He gave in order to the Mysteries,
The Sky, the Earth, the Winds, as was their
        due.
"Before I eat, I offer this to you,"
He chanted as he gave; "so all men should.
I hope that what I eat may do me good,
And what you eat may help you even so.
I ask you now to make my children grow
To men and women. Keep us healthy still,
And give us many buffalo to kill
And plenty grass for animals to eat."

Some youths came forth to parcel out the meat
In order as the councillors were great
In deeds of worth; and each, before he ate,
Addressed the mystic sources of the good.

The feast now being finished, Red Cloud stood
Still pondering his words with mouth set grim;
But men felt thunder in the hush of him
And knew what lightning struggled to be wise
Behind the hawklike brooding of the eyes,
The chipped flint look about the cheek and jaw.
The humming of a hustling autumn flaw
In aspen thickets swept the waiting crowd.
It seemed his voice would tower harsh and loud.
It crooned.

      "My friends, 'twas many snows ago
When first we welcomed white men. Now we
    know
Their hearts are bad and all their words are
    lies.
They brought us shining things that pleased
    the eyes
And weapons that were better than we knew.
And this seemed very good. They brought us
    too
The spirit water, strong to wash away
The coward's fear, and for a moment stay
The creeping of old age and gnawing sorrow.
My friends, if you would have these things
    tomorrow,
Forget the way our fathers taught us all.
As though you planned to live till mountains
    fall,

Seek out all things men need and pile them high.
Be fat yourself and let the hungry die;
Be warm yourself and let the naked freeze.
So shall you see the trail the white man sees.
And when your tepee bulges to the peak,
Look round you for some neighbor who is weak
And take his little too. Dakotas, think!
Shall all the white man's trinkets and his
        drink,
By which the mind is overcome and drowned,
Be better than our homes and hunting ground,
The guiding wisdom of our old men's words?
Shall we be driven as the white man's herds
From grass to bitter grass? When Harney
        said
His people, seeking for the yellow lead,
Would like an iron trail across our land,
Our good old chieftains did not understand
What snake would crawl among us. It would
        pass
Across our country; not a blade of grass
Should wither for that passing, they were told.
And now when scarce the council fire is cold,
Along the Little Piney hear the beat
Of axes and the desecrating feet
Of soldiers! Are we cowards? Shall we stand
Unmoved as trees and see our Mother Land
Plowed up for corn?"

                    Increasing as he spoke,
The smothered wrath now mastered him, and
        'woke
The sleeping thunder all had waited for.
Out of a thrilling hush he shouted: "*War!*"—

A cry to make an enemy afraid.
The grazing ponies pricked their ears and
    neighed,
Recalling whirlwind charges; and the town
Roared after like a brush-jam breaking down
With many waters.

                When the quiet fell
Another rose with phrases chosen well
To glut the tribal wrath, and took his seat
Amid the crowd's acclaim. Like chunks of
    meat,
Flung bloody to a pack, raw words were said
By others; and the rabble's fury, fed,
Outgrew the eager feeding. Who would dare
To rise amid the blood-lust raging there
And offer water?

              Spotted Tail stood up;
And since all knew no blood was in the cup
That he would give, dumb scorn rejected him.
He gazed afar, and something seen made
    dim
The wonted quizzic humor of the eyes.
The mouth, once terrible with battle-cries,
Took on a bitter droop as he began.

"*Hey—hey'-hey!* So laments an aging man
Who totters and can never more be free
As once he was. *Hey—hey'-hey!* So may we
Exclaim today for what the morrow brings.
There is a time, my brothers, for all things,
And we are getting old. Consider, friends,
How everything begins and grows and ends
[29]

That other things may have their time and
grow.
What tribes of deer and elk and buffalo
Have we ourselves destroyed lest we should
die!
About us now you hear the dead leaves sigh;
Since these were green, how few the moons
have been!
We share in all this trying to begin,
This trying not to die. Consider well
The White Man—what you know and what
men tell
About his might. His never weary mind
And busy hands do magic for his kind.
Those things he loves we think of little worth;
And yet, behold! he sweeps across the earth,
And what shall stop him? Something that is
true
Must help him do the things that he can do,
For lies are not so mighty. Be not stirred
By thoughts of vengeance and the burning
word!
Such things are for the young; but let us give
Good counsel for the time we have to live,
And seek the better way, as old men should."

He ended; yet a little while he stood
Abashed and lonely, seeing how his words
Had left as little trace as do the birds
Upon the wide insouciance of air.
He sat at length; and round him crouching
there
The hostile silence closed, as waters close
Above the drowned.

                    Then Sitting Bull arose;
And through the stirring crowd a murmur 'woke
As of a river yielding to the stroke
Of some deft swimmer. No heroic height
Proclaimed him peer among the men of might,
Nor was his bearing such as makes men serve.
Bull-torsed, squat-necked, with legs that kept
        a curve
To fit the many ponies he had backed,
He scarcely pleased the eyes. But what he
        lacked
Of visible authority to mould
Men's lives, was compensated manifold
By something penetrating in his gaze
That searched the rabble, seeming to appraise
The common weakness that should make him
        strong.
One certainty about him held the throng—
His hatred of the white men. Otherwise,
Conjecture, interweaving truth and lies,
Wrought various opinions of the man.
A mountebank—so one opinion ran—
A battle-shirking intimate of squaws,
A trivial contriver of applause,
A user of the sacred for the base.
Yet there was something other in his face
Than vanity and craft. And there were those
Who saw him in that battle with the Crows
The day he did a thing no coward could.
There ran a slough amid a clump of wood
From whence, at little intervals, there broke
A roaring and a spurt of rifle-smoke
That left another wound among the Sioux.
Now Sitting Bull rode down upon the slough

To see what might be seen there.   What he saw
Was such as might have gladdened any squaw—
A wounded warrior with an empty gun!
'Twas then that deed of Sitting Bull was done,
And many saw it plainly from the hill.
Would any coward shun an easy kill
And lose a scalp? Yet many saw him throw
His loaded rifle over to the Crow,
Retreat a space, then wheel to charge anew.
With but a riding quirt he counted *coup*
And carried back a bullet in his thigh.
Let those who jeered the story for a lie
Behold him limping yet! And others said
He had the gift of talking with the dead
And used their clearer seeing to foretell
Dark things aright; that he could weave a spell
To make a foeman feeble if he would.

Such things the people pondered while he stood
And searched them with a quiet, broad-
      browed stare.
Then suddenly some magic happened there.
Can men grow taller in a breathing span?
He spoke; and even scorners of the man
Were conscious of a swift, disarming thrill,
The impact of a dominating will
That overcame them.

                              "Brothers, you have seen
The way the spring sun makes the prairie green
And wakes new life in animal and seed,
Preparing plenty for the biggest need,
Remembering the little hungers too.
The same mysterious quickening makes new

Men's hearts, for by that power we also live.
And so, till now, we thought it good to give
All life its share of what that power sends
To man and beast alike. But hear me, friends!
We face a greedy people, weak and small
When first our fathers met them, now grown
      tall
And overbearing. Tireless in toil,
These madmen think it good to till the soil,
And love for endless getting marks them fools.
Behold, they bind their poor with many rules
And let their rich go free! They even steal
The poor man's little for the rich man's weal!
Their feeble have a god their strong may flout!
They cut the land in pieces, fencing out
Their neighbors from the mother of all men!
When she is sick, they make her bear again
With medicines they give her with the seed!
All this is sacrilegious! Yet they heed
No word, and like a river in the spring
They flood the country, sweeping everything
Before them! 'Twas not many snows ago
They said that we might hunt our buffalo
In this our land forever. Now they come
To break that promise. Shall we cower,
      dumb?
Or shall we say: 'First kill us—here we
      stand!'"

He paused; then stooping to the mother-land,
He scraped a bit of dust and tossed it high.
Against the hollow everlasting sky
All watched it drifting, sifting back again
In utter silence. "So it is with men,"

Said Sitting Bull, his voice now low and tense;
"What better time, my friends, for going
    hence
Than when we have so many foes to kill?"

He ceased. As though they heard him speak-
    ing still,
The people listened; for he had a way
That seemed to mean much more than he
    could say
And over all the village cast a spell.
At length some warrior uttered in a yell
The common hate. 'Twas like the lean blue
    flash
That stabs a sultry hush before the crash
Of heaven-rending thunder and the loud
Assault of winds. Then fury took the crowd
And set it howling with the lust to slay.

The councillors were heard no more that day;
And from the moony hill tops all night long
The wolves gave answer to the battle-song,
And saw their valley hunting-grounds aflare
With roaring fires, and frenzied shadows there
That leaped and sang as wolves do, yet were
    men.

IV. FORT PHIL KEARNEY

Long since the column, pushing north again
With Carrington, had left the little post
On Laramie; unwitting how the ghost
Of many a trooper, lusty yet and gay,
Disconsolately drifting back that way,
Should fill unseen the gaps of shattered ranks.

Scarce moved to know what shadows dogged
    their flanks,
Till all the winds that blew were talking spies
And draws had ears and every hill-top, eyes,
And silence, tongues, the seven hundred
    went.
How brazenly their insolent intent
Was flaunted! Even wolves might under-
    stand
These men were going forth to wed the land
And spawn their breed therein. Behold their
    squaws!
Could such defend the Great White Father's
    laws?
So weak they were their warriors hewed the
    wood,
Nor did they tend the pots, as women should,
Nor fill them.

           Powder River caught the word
Of how they swam their long-horned cattle herd

At Bridger's Ferry. Big Horn and the Tongue
Beheld through nearer eyes the long line flung
Up Sage Creek valley; heard through distant
    ears
The cracking lashes of the muleteers
The day the sandy trail grew steep and bleak.
The Rosebud saw them crossing Lightning
    Creek,
Whence, southward, cone outsoaring dizzy
    cone,
Until the last gleamed splendidly alone,
They viewed the peak of Laramie. When, high
Between the head of North Fork and the Dry
They lifted Cloud Peak scintillant with snows,
The Cheyenne hunters and Arapahoes,
Far-flung as where the Wind becomes the Horn,
Discussed their progress. Spirits of the morn,
That watched them break the nightly camp
    and leave,
Outwinged the crane to gossip with the eve
In distant camps. Beyond the Lodge Pole's
    mouth
Relentless Red Cloud, poring on the south,
Could see them where the upper Powder ran
Past Reno Post, and counted to a man
The soldiers left there. Tattlings of the noon
Were bruited by the glimmer of the moon
In lands remote; till, pushing northward yet
Past Crazy Woman's Fork and Lake DeSmedt,
They reached the Big and Little Piney Creeks.

Some such a land the famished hunter seeks
In fever-dreams of coolness. All day long
The snow-born waters hummed a little song

To virgin meadows, till the sun went under;
Then tardy freshets in a swoon of thunder,
That deepened with the dark, went rushing by,
As 'twere the Night herself sang lullaby
Till morning. Cottonwoods and evergreens
Made music out of what the silence means
In timeless solitudes. And over all,
White towers dizzy on a floating wall
Of stainless white, the Big Horn Mountains
        rose.
Absoraka, the Country of the Crows,
A land men well might fight for!

                          Here they camped,
Rejoicing, man and beast. The work-mule
        champed
The forage of the elk, and rolled to sate
His lust for greenness. Like a voice of fate,
Foretelling ruthless years, his blatant bray
With horns of woe and trumpets of dismay
Crowded the hills. The milk cow and the steer
In pastures of the bison and the deer
Lowed softly. And the trail-worn troopers
        went
About their duties, whistling, well content
To share this earthly paradise of game.

But scarcely were the tents up, when there
        came—
Was it a sign? One moment it was noon,
A golden peace hypnotic with the tune
Of bugs among the grasses; and the next,
The spacious splendor of the world was vexed
With twilight that estranged familiar things.
A moaning sound, as of enormous wings

Flung wide to bear some swooping bat of death,
Awakened. Hills and valleys held their breath
To hear that sound. A nervous troop-horse neighed
  neighed
Shrill in the calm. Instinctively afraid,
The cattle bellowed and forgot to graze;
And raucous mules deplored the idle day's
Untimely end. Then presently there fell
What seemed a burlesque blizzard out of hell—
A snow of locusts—tawny flakes at strife,
That, driven by a gust of rabid life,
Smothered the windless noon! The lush grass bent,
  bent,
Devoured in bending. Wagon-top and tent
Sagged with the drift of brown corrosive snow.
Innumerable hungers shrilled below;
A humming fog of hungers hid the sky,
Until a cool breath, falling from the high
White ramparts, came to cleanse the stricken world.
  world.
Then suddenly the loud rack lifted, swirled
To eastward; and the golden light returned.

Now day by day the prairie people learned
What wonders happened where the Pineys flowed;
  flowed;
How many wagons rutted out a road
To where the pines stood tallest to be slain;
What medicine the White Man's hand and brain
  brain
Had conjured; how they harnessed up a fog
That sent a round knife screaming through a log
From end to end; how many adzes hewed;
And how the desecrated solitude

Beheld upon a level creek-side knoll
The rise of fitted bole on shaven bole,
Until a great fort brazened out the sun.
And while that builded insolence was done,
Far prairies saw the boasting banner flung
Above it, like a hissing adder's tongue,
To menace every ancientry of good.

Long since and oft the workers in the wood
Had felt the presence of a foe concealed.
The drone of mowers in the haying-field
Was silenced often by the rifle's crack,
The arrow's whirr; and often, forging back
With lash and oath along the logging road,
The scared mule-whacker fought behind his
    load,
His team a kicking tangle. Oft by night
Some hill top wagged a sudden beard of light,
Immediately shorn; and dark hills saw
To glimmer sentient. Hours of drowsy awe
Near dawn had heard the raided cattle bawl,
Afraid of alien herdsmen; bugles call
To horse; the roaring sally; fleeing cries.
And oft by day upon a distant rise
Some naked rider loomed against the glare
With hand at brow to shade a searching
    stare,
Then like a dream dissolved in empty sky.

So men and fate had labored through July
To make a story. August browned the plain;
And ever Fort Phil Kearney grew amain
With sweat of toil and blood of petty fights.
September brought the tingling silver nights

[39]

And men worked faster, thinking of the snows.
Aye, more than storm they dreaded. Friendly
    Crows
Had told wild tales. Had they not ridden
    through
The Powder River gathering of Sioux?
And lo, at one far end the day was young;
Noon saw the other! Up along the Tongue
Big villages were dancing! Everywhere
The buzzing wasp of war was in the air.

October smouldered goldenly, and gray
November sulked and threatened. Day by day,
While yet the greater evils held aloof,
The soldiers wrought on wall, stockade and roof
Against the coming wrath of God and Man.
And often where the lonely home-trail ran
They gazed with longing eyes; nor did they see
The dust cloud of the prayed-for cavalry
And ammunition train long overdue.
By now they saw their forces cut in two,
First Reno Post upon the Powder, then
Fort Smith upon the Big Horn needing men;
And here the center of the brewing storm
Would rage.

       Official suavities kept warm
The wire to Laramie—assurance bland
Of peace now reigning in the prairie land;
Attest the treaty signed! So said the mail;
But those who brought it up the Bozeman Trail
Two hundred miles, could tell of running
    fights,
Of playing tag with Terror in the nights

To hide by day. If peace was anywhere,
It favored most the growing graveyard there
Across the Piney under Pilot Hill.

December opened ominously still,
And scarce the noon could dull the eager
     fang
That now the long night whetted. Shod hoofs
     rang
On frozen sod. The tenuated whine
And sudden shrick of buzz-saws biting pine
Were heard far off unnaturally loud.
The six-mule log-teams labored in a cloud;
The drivers beat their breasts with aching
     hands.
As yet the snow held off; but prowling bands
Grew bolder. Weary night-guards on the walls
Were startled broad awake by wolf-like calls
From spots of gloom uncomfortably near;
And out across the crystal hemisphere
Weird yammerings arose and died away
To dreadful silence. Every sunny day
The looking-glasses glimmered all about.
So, clinging to the darker side of doubt,
Men took their boots to bed, nor slumbered
     soon.

It happened on the sixth December noon
That from a hill commanding many a mile
The lookout, gazing off to Piney Isle,
Beheld the log-train crawling up a draw
Still half way out. With naked eye he saw
A lazy serpent reeking in the glare
Of wintry sunlight. Nothing else was there

But empty country under empty skies.
Then suddenly it seemed a blur of flies
Arose from each adjacent gulch and break
And, swarming inward, swirled about the snake
That strove to coil amid the stinging mass.
One moment through the ill-adjusted glass
Vague shadows flitted; then the whirling specks
Were ponies with their riders at their necks,
Swung low. The lurching wagons spurted smoke;
The teams were plunging.

                    Frantic signals woke
The bugles at the fort, the brawl of men
Obeying "boots and saddles."

                       Once again
The sentry lifts his glass. 'Tis like a dream.
So very near the silent figures seem
A hand might almost touch them. Here they come
Hell-bent for blood—distorted mouths made dumb
With distance! One can see the muffled shout,
The twang of bow-thongs! Leaping fog blots out
The agitated picture—flattens, spreads.
Dull rumblings wake and perish. Tossing heads
Emerge, and ramrods prickle in the rack.
A wheel-mule, sprouting feathers at his back,
Rears like a clumsy bird essaying flight
And falls to vicious kicking. Left and right
Deflected hundreds wheel about and swing
To charge anew—tempestuous galloping

On cotton! Empty ponies bolt away
To turn and stare high-headed on the fray
With muted snorting at the deeds men do.
But listen how at last a sound breaks through
The deathly silence of the scene! Hurrah
For forty troopers roaring down the draw
With Fetterman! A cloud of beaten dust
Sent skurrying before a thunder-gust,
They round the hogback yonder. With a rush
They pierce the limpid curtain of the hush,
Quiescing in the picture. Hurry, men!
The rabid dogs are rushing in again!
Look! Hurry! No, they break midway! They
    see
The squadron dashing up. They turn, they flee
Before that pack of terriers—like rats!
Yell, yell, you lucky loggers—wave your hats
And thank the Captain that you've kept your
    hair!
Look how they scatter to the northward there,
Dissolving into nothing! Ply the spurs,
You fire-eaters! Catch that pack of curs
This side the Peno, or they'll disappear!
Look out! They're swooping in upon your rear!
Wherever did they come from? Look! Good
    God!
The breaks ahead belch ponies, and the sod
On every side sprouts warriors!

                   Holy Spoons!
The raw recruits have funked it! Turn, you
    loons,
You cowards! Can't you see the Captain's game
To face them with a handful? Shame! O shame!

They'll rub him out—turn back—that's not
    the way
We did it to the Johnnies many a day
In Dixie! Every mother's baby rides
As though it mattered if they saved their hides!
Their empty faces gulp the miles ahead.
Ride on and live to wish that you were dead
Back yonder where the huddled muskets spit
Against a sea!

       Now—now you're in for it!
Here comes the Colonel galloping like sin
Around the hill! Hurrah—they're falling in—
Good boys! It's little wonder that you ran.
I'm not ashamed to say to any man
I might have run.

       Ah, what a pretty sight!
Go on, go on and show 'em that you're white!
They're breaking now—you've got 'em on the
    run—
They're scattering! Hurrah!

       The fight was done;
No victory to boast about, indeed—
Just labor. Sweat today, tomorrow, bleed—
An incidental difference. And when
The jaded troopers trotted home again
There wasn't any cheering. Six of those
Clung dizzily to bloody saddle-bows;
And Bingham was the seventh and was dead;
And Bowers, with less hair upon his head
Than arrows in his vitals, prayed to die.
He did that night.

Now thirteen days went by
With neither snow nor foe; and all the while
The log-trains kept the road to Piney Isle.
Soon all the needed timber would be hauled,
The work be done. Then, snugly roofed and
    walled,
What need for men to fear? Some came to deem
The former mood of dread a foolish dream,
Grew mellow, thinking of the holidays
With time for laughter and a merry blaze
On every hearth and nothing much to do.
As for the bruited power of the Sioux,
Who doubted it was overdrawn a mite?
At any rate, they wouldn't stand and fight
Unless the odds were heavy on their side.
It seemed the Colonel hadn't any pride—
Too cautious. Look at Fetterman and Brown,
Who said they'd ride the whole Sioux nation
    down
With eighty men; and maybe could, by jing!
Both scrappers—not afraid of anything—
A pair of eagles hungering for wrens!

And what about a flock of butchered hens
In Peno valley not so long ago
But for the Colonel? Bowers ought to know;
Go ask him! Thus the less heroic jeered.
These Redskins didn't run because they feared;
'Twas strategy; they didn't fight our way.

Again it happened on the nineteenth day
The lookout saw the logging-train in grief;
And Captain Powell, leading the relief,
Returned without a single scratch to show.

The twentieth brought neither snow nor foe.
The morrow came—a peaceful, scarlet morn.
It seemed the homesick sun in Capricorn
Had found new courage for the homeward
    track
And, yearning out across the zodiac
To Cancer, brightened with the conjured scene
Of grateful hills and valleys flowing green,
Sweet incense rising from the rain-soaked
    sward,
And color-shouts of welcome to the Lord
And Savior.

       Ninety took the logging-road
That morning, happy that the final load
Would trundle back that day, and all be well.
But hardly two miles out the foemen fell
Upon them, swarming three to one. And so
Once more the hill-top lookout signalled woe
And made the fort a wasp-nest buzzing ire.

The rip and drawl of running musket fire,
The muffled, rhythmic uproar of the Sioux
Made plain to all that what there was to do
Out yonder gave but little time to waste.
A band of horse and infantry soon faced
The Colonel's quarters, waiting for the word.
Above the distant tumult many heard
His charge to Powell, leader of the band;
And twice 'twas said that all might under-
    stand
The need for caution: "Drive away the foe
And free the wagon-train; but do not go
Past Lodge Trail Ridge."

A moment's silence fell;
And many in the after-time would dwell
Upon that moment, little heeded then—
The ghostly horses and the ghostly men,
The white-faced wives, the gaping children's
    eyes
Grown big with wonder and a dread surmise
To see their fathers waiting giant-tall;
That mumbling voice of doom beyond the wall;
The ghastly golden pleasance of the air;
And Fetterman, a spectre, striding there
Before the Colonel, while the portals yawn.
As vivid as a picture lightning-drawn
Upon the night, that memory would flash,
More vivid for the swooping backward crash
Of gloom. 'Twas but the hinges of the gates
That shrieked that moment, while the eager
    Fates
Told off the waiting band and gloated: *Done!*
He asked for eighty—give him eighty-one!
Then Fetterman, unwitting how the rim
Of endless outer silence pressed on him
And all his comrades, spoke: "With deference
    due
To Captain Powell, Colonel, and to you,
I claim command as senior captain here."

So ever is the gipsy Danger dear
To Courage; so the lusty woo and wed
Their dooms, to father in a narrow bed
A song against the prosing after-years.

And now the restive horses prick their ears
And nicker to the bugle. Fours about,
They rear and wheel to line. The hillsides shout

Back to the party. Forward! Now it swings
High-hearted through the gate of common
    things
To where bright hazard, like a stormy moon,
Still gleams round Hector, Roland, Sigurd,
    Fionn;
And all the lost, horizon-hungry prows,
Eternal in contemporary nows,
Heave seaward yet.

              The Colonel mounts the wall,
And once again is heard his warning call:
"Relieve the wagon-train, but do not go
Past Lodge Trail Ridge." And Fetterman,
    below,
Turns back a shining face on him, and smiles
Across the gap that neither years nor miles
May compass now.

            A little farther still
They watched him skirt a westward-lying hill
That hid him from the train, to disappear.
"He'll swing about and strike them in the rear,"
The watchers said, "and have the logging crew
For anvil."

          Now a solitary Sioux
Was galloping in circles on a height
That looked on both the squadron and the
    fight—
The prairie sign for "many bison seen."
A lucky case-shot swept the summit clean,
And presently the distant firing ceased;
Nor was there sound or sight of man or beast
Outside for age-long minutes after that.

At length a logger, spurring up the flat,
Arrived with words of doubtful cheer to say.
The Indians had vanished Peno way;
The train was moving on to Piney Isle.
He had no news of Fetterman.

V. RUBBED OUT

Meanwhile
Where ran the Bozeman Road along the bleak
North slope of Lodge Trail Ridge to Peno
    Creek,
Big hopes were burning. Silence waited there.
The brown land, even as the high blue air,
Seemed empty. Yet the troubled crows that
    flew
Keen-eyed above the sunning valley knew
What made the windless slough-grass ripple
    so,
And how a multitude of eyes below
Were peering southward to the road-scarred
    rise
Where every covert was alive with eyes
That scanned the bare horizon to the south.

The white of dawn had seen the Peno's
    mouth
A-swarm with men—Cheyennes, Arapahoes,
Dakotas. When the pale-faced sun arose—
A spectre fleeing from a bath of blood—
It saw them like a thunder-fathered flood
Surge upward through the sounding sloughs
    and draws—
Afoot and mounted, veterans and squaws,
Youths new to war, the lowly and the
    great—
A thousand-footed, single-hearted hate

Flung fortward. Now their chanted battle-
    songs
Dismayed the hills. Now silent with their
    wrongs
They strode, the sullen hum of hoofs and feet,
Through valleys where aforetime life was sweet,
More terrible than songs or battle cries.

The sun had traversed half the morning skies
When, entering the open flat, they poured
To where the roadway crossed the Peno ford
Below the Ridge. Above them wheeled and
    pried
The puzzled crows, to learn what thing had
    died,
What carcass, haply hidden from the ken
Of birds, had lured so large a flock of men
Thus chattering with lust. There, brooding
    doom,
They paused and made the brown December
    bloom
With mockeries of August—demon flowers
And lethal, thirsting for the sanguine showers
That soon should soak the unbegetting fields—
The trailing bonnets and the pictured shields,
The lances nodding in the warwind's breath,
And faces brave with paint to outstare Death
In some swift hush of battle!

                              Briefly so
They parleyed. Then the spears began to
    flow
On either side the Ridge—a double stream
Of horsemen, winking out as in a dream

High up among the breaks that flanked the trail.
Amid the tall dry grasses of the vale
The footmen disappeared; and all the place
Was still and empty as a dead man's face
That sees unmoved the wheeling birds of prey.

The anxious moments crawled. Then far away
Across the hills a muffled tumult grew,
As of a blanket being ripped in two
And many people shouting underground.
The valley grasses rippled to the sound
As though it were a gusty wind that passed.

Far off a bugle's singing braved the vast
And perished in a wail.

                              The tall grass stirred.

The rumor of the distant fight was heard
A little longer. Suddenly it stopped;
And silence, like a sky-wide blanket, dropped
Upon the landscape empty as the moon.

The sun, now scarce a lance-length from the
        noon,
Seemed waiting for whatever might occur.
Across the far Northwest a purplish blur
Had gathered and was crawling up the sky.

Now presently a nearer bugle cry
Defied the hush—a scarlet flower of sound
That sowed the sterile silences around
With futile seed of music.

                              Once again
The sound of firing and the cries of men

Arose; but now 'twas just beyond the place
Where, climbing to the azure rim of space,
The roadway topped the Ridge and disap-
    peared.
The tongueless coverts listened, thousand-
    eared,
And heard hoof-thunders rumbling over there.

Then suddenly the high blue strip of air
Was belching warriors in a wind of cries.
In breakneck rout they tumbled from the skies,
Wheeled round to fling more arrows at a foe,
And fled to where the breast-deep grass below
Swayed wildly.

                    Now a crow-black stallion 'rose,
And looming huge against the blue noon doze,
Raced back and forth across the Ridge's rim,
While, shooting from beneath the neck of him,
The Cheyenne Big Nose held the roaring rear;
Nor did the snarling musket-balls come near,
So mighty was his medicine, they say.
Now presently the high blue wall of day
Spewed cavalry along the Ridge; and then
A marvel for the tongues and ears of men
Amazed the hidden watchers of the height.
For like a thunder-stridden wind of night
That rages through a touselled poplar grove,
The rider of the stallion charged, and drove
Straight through the middle of the mounted
    crowd.
Men saw his bonnet tossing in a cloud
Of manes and tails; and sabre lightnings played
About it. Then, emerging undismayed,

He charged back through and galloped down
    the hill
With bullets that were impotent to kill
Spat-pinging all around.

                       The firing ceased.
The fugitives were half a mile at least
Beyond the Peno ford. There, circling wide
With bows and lances brandished, they defied
The foe to come and fight with them. By now
The infantry had crossed the Ridge's brow.
It joined the troop a little way below;
Then all together, cautiously and slow,
Came down the hated road. And silence lay
On summit, slope and valley, deep as day
And doomful, as they came. The flat could hear
The murmur of the straining saddle-gear,
The shuffling feet, the clinking of the bits;
And when a nervous troop-horse neighed by fits,
The ponies, lurking in the broken lands
That flanked the Ridge, kept silence for the
    hands
That gripped their nostrils.

                    Now the eighty-one
Were half way down the hill. The nooning sun
Slipped fearfully behind a flying veil,
And from the gray northwest a raw-cold gale
Came booming up. The fugitive decoys,
Off yonder in the flat, like playing boys
Divided now and waged a mimic fight.
Immediately half way up the height
Among the breaks appeared a warrior's torse.
A thousand hidden eyes knew Little Horse,

The Cheyenne chieftain; saw him wave a spear
Left-handed; pass it round him in the rear
To seize it with the right.

               The whole flat swarmed
With footmen.   Mounted warriors thunder-
    stormed
By hundreds from the breaks above; and one
Came dashing down the ridge-road at a run
And plunged among the soldiery to die
Beneath the frantic sabres. With a cry
That set the horses wild, the swarm closed in.

The cavalry, as hoping yet to win
The summit of the Ridge, wheeled round and
    hewed
A slow way upward through the solitude
Of lances, howling in the arrow-storm.
The rest, already circled by the swarm,
Took cover in a patch of tumbled rock
Where, huddled like a blizzard-beaten flock,
They faced the swirling death they could not
    stem.
A little while before it smothered them
The dwindling few toiled mightily, men say,
With gun-butts swinging in the dim mêlée
Of battle-clubs and lances; then were still.

The wave broke over, surging up the hill;
For yonder yet the battle smoked and roared
Where, midway 'twixt the summit and the ford,
The little band of troopers held the height—
Green manhood withering in a locust flight
Of arrows! Aye, a gloaming of despair
The shuttling arrows wove above them there,

[55]

So many were the bows. Cheyenne and Sioux
Went down beneath the shafts their brothers
        drew;
Arapahoes struck down Arapahoes
Unwittingly. And many a red gout froze
Along the slopes, so keen had grown the gale.

A little while those makers of a tale
Gave battle like a badger in a hole;
Nor could the ponies charge the narrow knoll,
For either slope was steep and gully-scrawled.
Still up and up the cautious bowmen crawled,
And still the troopers overawed the field.

Then presently, men say, a white chief reeled;
Rolled from his saddle; like a man gone daft
Got up and doddered, tugging at a shaft
That sprouted from his belly. Then a yell
Of many bowmen mocked him as he fell,
His writhing body feathered like a goose.

The troops began to turn their horses loose,
Retreating up the ridge, a hopeless crowd.
A lull of battle thinned the arrow-cloud
Above them; for the mounted warriors knew
The soldiers doomed whatever they might do,
And fell to rounding up the runaways.
Meanwhile the broken troopers in a daze
Of desperation scrambled up the slope.
Strewn boulders yonder woke a lying hope,
And there they waited, living, in their grave.

The horse-chase ended. Once again the wave
Began to mount the steep on either side,
While warriors hailed their fellows and replied:
Be ready!—We are ready, brothers!

Then
The hillsides bellowed with a surf of men
Flung crowding on the boulders. 'Twas the end.

Some trooper's wolfhound, mourning for his
    friend,
Loped fortward, pausing now and then to cry
His urgent question to the hostile sky
That spat a stinging frost. And someone said:
"Let yonder dog bear tidings of the dead
To make the white men tremble over there."
"No, teach them that we do not even spare
Their dogs!" another said. An arrow sang
Shrill to the mark. The wolfhound yelped
    and sprang,
Snapped at the feather, wilted, and was still.

And so they perished on that barren hill
Beside the Peno. And the Winter strode
Numb-footed down that bloody stretch of road
At twilight, when a squadron came to read
The corpse-writ rune of battle, deed by deed,
Between the Ridge's summit and the ford.

The blizzard broke at dusk. All night it roared
Round Fort Phil Kearney mourning for the
    slain.

VI. THE WAGON BOXES

Besieging January made the plain
One vast white camp to reinforce the foe
That watched the fort. Mad cavalries of snow
Assaulted; stubborn infantries of cold
Sat round the walls and waited. Wolves grew
    bold
To peer by night across the high stockade
Where, builded for the Winter's escalade,
The hard drifts leaned. And often in the
    deep
Of night men started from a troubled sleep
To think the guards were fighting on the wall
And, roaring over like a waterfall,
The wild hordes pouring in upon the lost.
But 'twas the timber popping in the frost,
The mourning wolves. Nor did the dawn
    bring cheer.
Becandled like a corpse upon a bier
The lifeless sun, from gloom to early gloom,
Stole past,—a white procession to a tomb
Illumining the general despair.

Meanwhile Omniscience in a swivel chair,
Unmenaced half a continent away,
Amid more pressing matters of the day
Had edited the saga of the dead.
Compare the treaty where it plainly said

There was no war! All duly signed and sealed!
Undoubtedly the evidence revealed
The need of an official reprimand.
Wherefore stern orders ticked across the land
From Washington to Laramie. Perhaps
No blizzard swept the neat official maps
To nip a tracing finger. Howsoe'er,
Four companies of horse and foot must bear
To Fort Phil Kearney tidings of its shame.
Through ten score miles of frozen hell they
    came—
Frost-bitten, wolfish—with the iron word
Of Carrington dishonored and transferred
To Reno Post. The morning that he went,
The sun was like a sick man in a tent,
Crouched shivering between two feeble fires.
Far off men heard his griding wagon tires
Shriek fife-like in the unofficial snow,
His floundering three-span mule-teams blaring
    woe
Across the blue-cold waste; and he was gone.

Without a thaw the bitter spell wore on
To raging February. Days on days
Men could not see beyond the whirling haze
That made the fort's the world's wall fronting
    sheer
On chaos. When at times the sky would clear
And like a frozen bubble were the nights,
Pale rainbows jigged across the polar heights
And leafy rustlings mocked the solitude.
Men sickened with the stale and salty food,
For squadrons hunt at best with ill success;
And quiet days revealed the wilderness

Alert with fires, so doggedly the foe
Guarded the deer and elk and buffalo
That roamed the foothills where the grass was
     good.
A battle often bought a load of wood;
And arrows swept the opening water-gate
From where the wily bowmen lurked in wait
Along the brush-clad Piney.

                   March went past,
A lion, crouched or raging, to the last;
And it was April—in the almanac.
No maiden with the southwind at her back
Ran crocus-footed up the Bozeman Road.
A loveless vixen swept her drear abode
With brooms of whimsic wrath, and scolded
     shrill.
Men pined to think of how the whippoorwill
Broidered the moony silences at home.
There now a mist-like green began to roam
The naked forest hillward from the draws;
The dogwood's bloom was vying with the
     haw's;
The redbud made a bonfire of its boughs.
And there, perchance, one lying in a drowse
At midnight heard the friendly thunder crash,
The violet-begetting downpour lash
The flaring panes; and possibly one heard
The sudden rapture of a mocking bird
Defy the lightning in a pitch-black lull.

Here dull days wore the teeth of Winter dull.
Drifts withered slowly. Of an afternoon
The gulches grumbled hoarsely, ceasing soon

When sunset faded out. The pasque flower
    broke
The softened sod, and in a furry cloak
And airy bonnet brazened out the chill.
The long grave yonder under Pilot Hill,
Where eighty lay, was like a wound un-
    wrapped.
The cottonwoods, awaking sluggish-sapped,
Prepared for spring with wavering belief.
May stole along the Piney like a thief.

And yet, another sun made summer now
In wild hearts given glebe-like to the plow
Of triumph. So miraculously fed
With slaughter, richly seeded with the dead,
The many-fielded harvest throve as one.

And Red Cloud was the summer and the sun.

In many a camp, in three great tribal tongues,
That magic name was thunder in the lungs
Of warriors. Swift, apocalyptic light,
It smote the zenith of the Red Man's night
With dazzling vision. Forts dissolved in smoke,
The hated roadway lifted, drifted, broke
And was a dust; the white men were a tale;
The green, clean prairie bellowed, hill and vale,
With fatted bison; and the good old days
Came rushing back in one resistless blaze
Of morning!

        It was good to be a youth
That season when all dreaming was the truth
And miracle familiar! Waning May
Could hear the young men singing on the way

To Red Cloud. Pious sons and rakehell scamps,
Unbroken colts, the scandals of their camps,
And big-eyed dreamers never tried by strife,
One-hearted with the same wild surge of life,
Sang merrily of dying as they came.
Aloof amid his solitude of fame,
The battle-brooding chieftain heard, to dream
Of great hordes raging like a flooded stream
From Powder River to the Greasy Grass,
That never after might a wagon pass
Along that hated highway of deceit.

The meadows of Absoraka grew sweet
With nursing June. War-ponies, winter-thin,
Nuzzled the dugs of ancient might therein
Against the day of victory. July
Poured virile ardor from a ruthless sky
To make stern forage—that the hardened herds
Might speed as arrows, wheel and veer as birds,
Have smashing force and never lack for breath,
Be fit for bearing heroes to their death
In that great day now drawing near.

                                    Meanwhile
Once more the solitude of Piney Isle
Was startled with a brawl of mules and men.
The Long Knives' wagons clattered there again;
The axes bit and rang, saws whined and gnawed;
And mountain valleys wakened to applaud
The mighty in their downfall, meanly slain.

Now close to Piney Isle there lay a plain
Some three long bow-shots wide. Good graz-
    ing land
It was, and empty as a beggar's hand.

Low foothills squatted round with bended
    knees,
And standing mountains waited back of these
To witness what the hunkered hills might view.
They saw a broad arena roofed with blue
That first of August.   Where the mid-plain
    raised
A little knoll, the yellow swelter blazed
On fourteen wagon-beds set oval-wise—
A small corral to hold the camp supplies,
Flour, salt, beans, ammunition, grain in sacks.
Therein, forestalling sudden night attacks,
The mules were tethered when the gloaming
    starred
The laggard evening.   Soldiers, sent to guard
The logging crew, had pitched their tents
    around.
And all of this was like a feeble sound
Lost in the golden fanfare of the day.
Across the Piney Fork, a mile away,
Unseen among the pines, the work-camp stood;
And trundling thence with loads of winter wood,
Stript wagon-trucks creaked fortward.

                  Twilight awe
Among the pines now silenced axe and saw.
With jingling traces, eager for their grain,
Across the creek and up the gloaming plain
The work mules came, hee-hawing at the glow
Of fires among the tents.   The day burned low
To moonless dusk. The squat hills seemed to lift,
Expectant.   Peaks on shadow-seas adrift,
Went voyaging where lonely wraiths of cloud
Haunted the starry hushes.   Bugs grew loud

Among the grasses; cynic owls laughed shrill;
Men slept. But all night long the wolves were
    still,
Aware of watchers in the outer dark.
And now and then a sentry's dog would bark,
Rush snarling where it seemed that nothing
    stirred.
But those who listened for a war-cry, heard
The skirling bugs, the jeering owls, the deep
Discordant snoring of the men asleep
Upon their guns, mules blowing in the hay.

At last the blanching summits saw the day.
A drowsy drummer spread the news of morn.
The mules began to nicker for their corn
And wrangle with a laying back of ears.
Among them went the surly muleteers,
Dispensing feed and sulphurous remarks.
The harness rattled, and the meadow larks
Set dawn to melody. A sergeant cried
The names of heroes. Common men replied,
Sing-songing down the line. The squat hills
    heard
To seize and gossip with the running word—
Here! Here! Here! Coffee steaming in the pot,
Wood-smoke and slabs of bacon, sizzling hot,
Were very good to smell. The cook cried
    "chuck!"
And when the yellow flood of sunrise struck
The little prairie camp, it fell on men
Who ate as though they might not eat again.
Some wouldn't, for the day of wrath arose.
And yet, but for a cruising flock of crows,
The basking world seemed empty.

Now the sun
Was two hours high. The axes had begun
Across the Piney yonder. Drowsy draws
Snored with the lagging echoes of the saws.
The day swooned windless, indolently meek.
It happened that the pickets by the creek
Were shaken from a doze by rhythmic cries
And drumming hoofs. Against the western
    skies,
Already well within a half a mile,
Came seven Indians riding single file,
Their wiry ponies flattened to the quirt.
A sentry's Springfield roared, and hills, alert
With echoes, fired a ghostly enfillade.
The ball fell short, bit dust and ricocheted.
The foremost pony, smitten in the breast,
Went down amid the rearing of the rest
And floundered to a dusty somersault.
Unhurt, the tumbled brave emerged to vault
Behind a comrade; and the seven veered
To southward, circling round the spot they
    feared
Where three far-stinging human hornets stood.
Now one of these went running to the wood
To see what made the logging camp so
    still.
Short breath sufficed to tell the tale of ill
He brought—the whole crew making off in
    stealth
And going to the mountains for their health,
The mules stampeded!

                    Things were looking blue.
With shaking knees, uncertain what to do,

The pickets waited. Whisperings of death
Woke round them, and they felt the gusty
        breath
Of shafts that plunked and quivered in the sod.
As though men sprouted where the ponies trod,
The circling band now jeered them, ten to one.
They scanned the main camp swinking in the
        sun.
No signal to return! But all the men
Were rushing round there, staring now and then
To where the foothills, northward, broke the
        flat.

A pointing sentry shouted: "Look at that!
Good God! There must be thousands over
        there!"
Massed black against the dazzle of the air,
They made the hilltops crawlingly alive—
The viscid boiling over of a hive
That feels the pale green burning of the spring.
Slow-moving, with a phasic murmuring
As of a giant swarm gone honey-wild,
They took the slope; and still the black rear
        piled
The wriggling ridges. What could bar the way?
Dwarfed in the panorama of the day,
The camp was but a speck upon the plain.
And three remembered eighty lying slain
Beside a ford, and how the Winter strode
Numb-footed down a bloody stretch of road
Across strange faces lately known and dear.

"I guess we'd better hustle out of here,"
The sergeant said. To left, to right, in front,
Like starving kiotes singing to the hunt,

Yet overcautious for a close attack,
Scores pressed the fighting trio, falling back
Across the Piney campward. One would pause
To hold the rear against the arrow-flaws,
The pelting terror, while the two ran past;
Then once again the first would be the last,
The second, first. And still the shuttling hoofs
Wove closelier with gaudy warps and woofs
The net of death; for still from brush and break
The Piney, like a pregnant water snake,
Spewed venomous broods.

                So fleeing up the slope
The pickets battled for the bitter hope
Of dying with their friends. And there was one
Who left the wagon boxes at a run
And, dashing past the now exhausted three,
Knelt down to rest his rifle on his knee
And coolly started perforating hides.
Bare ponies, dragging warriors at their sides
And kicking at the unfamiliar weight,
Approved his aim. The weaving net of hate
Went loose, swung wide to southward.

                       So at last
They reached the camp where, silent and
    aghast,
The men stood round and stared with haunted
    eyes.
'Tis said a man sees much before he dies.
Were these not dying? O the eighty-one
Bestrewn down Lodge Trail Ridge to Peno Run
That blizzard evening! Here were thirty-two!
And no one broached what everybody knew—

The tale there'd be and maybe none to tell
But glutted crows and kiotes. Such a spell
As fastens on a sick room gripped the crowd—
When tick by tick the doctor's watch is loud,
With hours between. And like the sound of
    leaves
Through which a night-wind ominously grieves,
The murmur of that moving mass of men
To northward rose and fell and rose again,
More drowsing music than a waking noise.

And Captain Powell spoke: "Get ready, boys;
Take places; see their eyes, then shoot to kill."

Some crouched behind the boxes, staring still
Like men enchanted. Others, seeming fain
To feel more keenly all that might remain
Of ebbing life, paced nervously about.
One fortified the better side of doubt
With yokes of oxen. That was Tommy Doyle.
(Alas, the total profit of his toil
Would be a hot slug crunching through his
    skull!)
And Littman yonder, grunting in the lull,
Arranged a keg of salt to fight behind;
While Condon, having other things in mind
Than dying, wrestled with a barrel of beans.
And others planned escape by grimmer means.
Old Robertson, with nothing in his face,
Unlaced a boot and noosed the leather lace
To reach between a trigger and a toe.
He did not tell, and no one asked to know
The meaning of it. Everybody knew.
John Grady and McQuarie did it too,

And Haggirty and Gibson did the same,
And many others. When the finish came,
At least there'd be no torturing for them.

Now as a hail-cloud, fraying at the hem,
Hurls ragged feelers to the windless void,
The nearing mass broke vanward and deployed
To left and right—a dizzy, flying blear,
Reek of a hell-pot boiling in the rear.
And now, as when the menaced world goes
      strange
And cyclone sling-shots, feeling out the range,
Spatter the waiting land agape with drouth,
The few first arrows fell. Once more the south
Was humming with a wind of mounted men
That wove the broken net of death again
Along the creek and up the campward rise.

Then suddenly, with wolfish battle-cries
And death-songs like the onset of a gale
And arrows pelting like a burst of hail,
The living tempest broke. There was no plain;
Just head-gear bobbing in a toss of mane,
And horses, horses, horses plunging under.
Paunch-deep in dust and thousand-footed
      thunder,
That vertigo of terror swarmed and swirled
About the one still spot in all the world—
The hushed cyclonic heart. Then that was loud!
The boxes bellowed, and a spurting cloud
Made twilight where the flimsy fortress stood;
And flying splinters from the smitten wood
And criss-cross arrows pricked the drifting
      haze.

Not now, as in the recent musket days,
The foe might brave two volleys for a rush
Upon the soldiers, helpless in a hush
Of loading. Lo, like rifles in a dream
The breech-fed Springfields poured a steady
    stream
That withered men and horses roaring in!
And gut-shot ponies screamed above the din;
And many a wounded warrior, under-trod
But silent, wallowed on the bloody sod—
Man piled on man and horses on the men!

They broke and scattered. Would they come
    again?
Abruptly so the muted hail-storm leaves
Astonished silence, when the dripping eaves
Count seconds for the havoc yet to come.
Weird in the hush, a melancholy hum,
From where the watching women of the Sioux
Thronged black along the circling summits,
    grew
And fell and grew—the mourning for the dead.

One whispered hoarsely from a wagon-bed,
"Is anybody hit?" But none replied.
Awe-struck at what they did and hollow-eyed,
All watched and waited for the end of things.

Then even as the fleeing hail-cloud swings
Before some freakish veering of the gale,
Returning down its desolated trail
With doubled wrath, the howling horsemen
    came.
Right down upon the ring of spurting flame

The quirted ponies thundered; reared, afraid
Of that bad medicine the white men made,
And, screaming, bolted off with flattened ears.
So close the bolder pressed, that clubs and spears
Were hurled against the ring.

                                    Again they broke,
To come again. Now flashing through the
        smoke,
Like lightning to the battle's thunder-shocks,
Ignited arrows, streaming to the nocks,
Fell hissing where the fighting soldiers lay;
And flame went leaping through the scattered
        hay
To set the dry mule-litter smouldering.

Half suffocated, coughing with the sting
Of acrid air, like scythemen in a field
The soldiers mowed. And gaudy man-flower
        reeled
To wriggling swaths. And still the mad Sioux
        fought
To break this magic that the white men
        wrought—
Heroic flesh at grapple with a god.

Then noon was glaring on the bloody sod;
And broken clouds of horsemen down the plain
Went scudding; hundreds, heavy with the slain
And wounded, lagging in the panic rout.

Again the ridges murmured round about
Where wailed the wives and mothers of the
        Sioux.
Some soldier whispered, asking for a chew,

As though he feared dread sleepers might arise.
Young Tommy Doyle with blood upon his eyes
Gaped noonward and his fighting jaw sagged
    loose.
Hank Haggirty would never need a noose
To reach between a trigger and a toe.
Jenness would never hear a bugle blow
Again, so well he slept. Around the ring
Men passed the grisly gossip, whispering—
As though doomed flesh were putting on the
    ghost.

A sound grew up as of a moving host.
It seemed to issue from a deep ravine
To westward. There no enemy was seen.
A freak gust, gotten of a sultry hush,
May mumble thus among the distant brush
Some moments ere a dampened finger cools.
But still the smudgy litter of the mules
Plumed straight against the dazzle of the day.
Upon a hilltop half a mile away
To eastward, Red Cloud presently appeared
Among his chieftains, gazing where the weird
Susurrus swelled and deepened in the west;
And to and from him dashed along the crest
Fleet heralds of some new-begotten hope.

Once more the Piney spread along the slope
A dizzy ruck of charging horse. They broke
Before those stingers in a nest of smoke,
Fled back across the creek, and waited there.
For what?

        The voice of it was everywhere—
A bruit of waters fretting at a weir.

The woman-peopled summits hushed to hear
That marching sound.

                         Then suddenly a roar,
As from the bursting open of a door,
Swept out across the plain; and hundreds,
       pressed
By hundreds crowding yonder from the west,
Afoot and naked, issued like a wedge,
With Red Cloud's nephew for the splitting edge,
A tribe's hot heart behind him for a maul.

Slow, ponderously slow, the V-shaped wall
Bore down upon the camp. The whirlwind pace
Of horsemen seemed less terrible to face
Than such a leisure. Brave men held their
       breath
Before that garish masquerade of Death
Aflaunt with scarlets, yellows, blues and greens.

Then Condon there behind his barrel of beans,
Foreseeing doom, afraid to be afraid,
Sprang up and waved his rifle and essayed
Homeric speech according to his lights.
"Come on!" he yelled, "ye dairty blatherskites,
Ye blitherin' ijuts! We kin lick yez all,
Ye low-down naygurs!" Shafts began to fall
About him raging. Scattered muskets roared
Along the fraying fringes of the horde.
"Get down there, Jim!" men shouted.
      "Down!" But Jim
Told Death, the blackguard, what he thought
       of him
For once and all.

Again the Springfields crashed;
And where the heavy bullets raked and smashed
The solid front and bored the jostling mass,
Men withered down like flame-struck prairie
    grass;
But still the raging hundreds forged ahead
Pell mell across their wounded and their dead,
Like tumblebugs. The splitting edge went
    blunt.
A momentary eddy at the front
Sucked down the stricken chief. The heavy
    rear,
With rage more mighty than the vanward fear,
Thrust forward. Twenty paces more, and
    then—
'Twould be like drowning in a flood of men.
Already through the rifts one saw their eyes,
Teeth flashing in the yawn of battle-cries,
The sweat-sleek muscles straining at the bows.

Forgotten were the nooses for the toes.
Tomorrows died and yesterdays were naught.
Sleep-walkers in a foggy nowhere fought
With shadows. So forever from the first,
Forever so until this dream should burst
Its thin-blown bubble of a world. And then,
The shadows were a howling mass of men
Hurled, heavy with their losses, down the plain
Before that thunder-spew of death and pain
That followed till the last had disappeared.
The hush appalled; and when the smoke had
    cleared,
Men eyed each other with a sense of shock
At being still alive.

'Twas one o'clock!

One spoke of water.   Impishly the word
Went round the oval, mocking those who heard.
The riddled barrel had bled from every stave;
And what the sun-stewed coffee-kettles gave
Seemed scarcely wet.
     Off yonder on the hill
Among his chieftains Red Cloud waited still—
A tomcat lusting for a nest of mice.
How often could these twenty-nine suffice
To check his thousands? Someone raised a sight
And cursed, and fell to potting at the height;
Then others.   Red Cloud faded into air.

What fatal mischief was he brewing there?
What ailed the Fort?   It seemed beyond belief
That Wessels yonder wouldn't send relief!
The hush bred morbid fancies.   Battle-cries
Were better than this buzzing of the flies
About Jenness and Haggirty and Doyle.
Wounds ached and smarted. Shaken films of oil
Troubled the yellow dazzle of the grass.
The bended heavens were a burning glass
Malevolently focussed.   Minutes crawled.
Men gnawed their hearts in silence where they
  sprawled,
Each in the puddle of his own blue shade.

But hear! Was that a howitzer that bayed?
Look!   Yonder from behind the eastward steep
Excited warriors, like a flock of sheep
That hear the wolves, throng down the creek-
  ward slope
And flee along the Piney!

[75]

Slow to hope,
Men searched each other's faces, silent still.

A case-shot, bursting yonder on the hill,
Sent dogging echoes up the foe-choked draws.
And far hills heard the leather-lunged hurrahs
And answered, when the long blue skirmish
        line
Swept down the hill to join the twenty-nine
Knee-deep in standing arrows.

VII. BEECHER'S ISLAND

                    Summer turned.
Where blackbirds chattered and the scrub oaks
        burned
In meadows of the Milk and Musselshell,
The fatted bison sniffed the winter-smell
Beneath the whetted stars, and drifted south.
Across the Yellowstone, lean-ribbed with
        drouth,
The living rivers bellowed, morn to morn.
The Powder and the Rosebud and the Horn
Flowed backward freshets, roaring to their
        heads.
Now up across the Cheyenne watersheds
The manless cattle wrangled day and night.
Along the Niobrara and the White
Uncounted thirsts were slaked. The peace
        that broods
Aloof among the sandhill solitudes
Fled from the bawling bulls and lowing
        cows.
Along the triple Loup they paused to browse
And left the lush sloughs bare. Along the
        Platte
The troubled myriads pawed the sandy flat
And snorted at the evil men had done.
For there, from morning sun to evening sun,
A strange trail cleft the ancient bison world,
And many-footed monsters whirred and
        whirled

Upon it; many-eyed they blinked, and screamed;
Tempestuous with speed, the long mane
    streamed
Behind them; and the breath of them was loud—
A rainless cloud with lightning in the cloud
And alien thunder.

               Thus the driving breed,
The bold earth-takers, toiled to make the deed
Audacious as the dream. One season saw
The steel trail crawl away from Omaha
As far as ox-rigs waddled in a day—
An inchworm bound for San Francisco Bay!
The next beheld a brawling, sweating host
Of men and mules build on to Kearney Post
While spring greens mellowed into winter
    browns,
And prairie dogs were giving up their towns
To roaring cities. Where the Platte divides,
The metal serpent sped, with league-long
    strides,
Between two winters. North Platte City sprang
From sage brush where the prairie sirens sang
Of magic bargains in the marts of lust;
A younger Julesburg sprouted from the dust
To howl a season at the panting trains;
Cheyenne, begotten of the ravished plains,
All-hailed the planet as the steel clanged by.
And now in frosty vacancies of sky
The rail-head waited spring on Sherman Hill,
And, brooding further prodigies of will,
Blinked off at China.

             So the man-stream flowed
Full flood beyond the Powder River road—

A cow path, hardly worth the fighting for.
Then let grass grow upon the trails of war,
Bad hearts be good and all suspicion cease!
Beside the Laramie the pipe of peace
Awaited; let the chieftains come and smoke!

'Twas summer when the Great White Father
  spoke.
A thousand miles of dying summer heard;
And nights were frosty when the crane-winged
  word
Found Red Cloud on the Powder loath to yield.
The crop from that rich seeding of the field
Along the Piney flourished greenly still.
The wail of many women on a hill
Was louder than the word.   And once again
He saw that blizzard of his fighting men
Avail as snow against the August heat.
"Go tell them I am making winter meat;
No time for talk," he said; and that was all.

The Northwind snuffed the torches of the fall,
And drearily the frozen moons dragged past.
Then when the pasque-flower dared to bloom
  at last
And resurrected waters hailed the geese,
It happened that the flying word of peace
Came north again.   The music that it made
Was sweet to Spotted Tail, and Man Afraid
Gave ear, bewitched.   One Horn and Little
  Chief
Believed; and Two Bears ventured on belief,
And others who were powers in the land.
For here was something plain to understand:

As long as grass should grow and water flow,
Between Missouri River and the snow
That never melts upon the Big Horn heights,
The country would be closed to all the Whites.
So ran the song that lured the mighty south.
It left a bitter taste in Red Cloud's mouth,
No music in his ears. "Go back and say
That they can take their soldier-towns away
From Piney Fork and Crazy Woman's Creek
And Greasy Grass. Then maybe I will speak.
Great Spirit gave me all this country here.
They have no land to give."

                          The hills went sere
Along the Powder; and the summer grew.
June knew not what the white men meant to do;
Nor did July. The end of August came.
Bullberries quickened into jets of flame
Where smoky bushes smouldered by the creeks.
Grapes purpled and the plums got rosy cheeks.
The nights were like a watching mother, yet
A chill as of incipient regret
Foretold the winter when the twilight fell.
'Twas then a story wonderful to tell
Went forth at last. In every wind it blew
Till all the far-flung bison hunters knew;
And Red Cloud's name and glory filled the tale.
The soldier-towns along the hated trail
Were smoke, and all the wagons and the men
Were dust blown south! Old times had come
     again.
Unscared, the fatted elk and deer would roam
Their pastures now, the bison know their home
And flourish there forever unafraid.

So when the victor's winter-meat was made
And all his lodges ready for the cold,
He listened to the word, now twelve moons old,
Rode south and made his sign and had his will.

Meanwhile the road along the Smoky Hill
Was troubled. Hunters, drifting with the herd
The fall before, had scattered wide the word
Of Red Cloud's victory. "Look north," they
        said;
The white men made a road there. It is red
With their own blood, and now they whine for
        peace!"
The brave tale travelled southward with the
        geese,
Nor dwindled on the way, nor lacked applause.
Comanches, South Cheyennes and Kiowas,
Apaches and the South Arapahoes
Were glad to hear. Satanta, Roman Nose,
Black Kettle, Little Raven heard—and thought.
Around their winter fires the warriors fought
Those far-famed battles of the North again.
Their hearts grew strong. "We, too," they
        said, "are men;
And what men did up yonder, we can do.
Make red the road along the Smoky too,
And grass shall cover it!"

                              So when the spring
Was fetlock-deep, wild news ran shuddering
Through Kansas: women captured, homes
        ablaze,
Men slaughtered in the country north of Hays
And Harker! Terror stalking Denver way!
Trains burned along the road to Santa Fe,

The drivers scalped and given to the flames!
All summer Panic babbled demon names.
No gloom but harbored Roman Nose, the Bat.
Satanta, like an omnipresent cat,
Moused every heart. Out yonder, over there,
Black Kettle, Turkey Leg were everywhere.
And Little Raven was the night owl's croon,
The watch-dog's bark. The setting of the moon
Was Little Rock; the dew before the dawn
A sweat of horror!

                All that summer, drawn
By vague reports and captive women's wails,
The cavalry pursued dissolving trails—
And found the hotwind. Loath to risk a fight,
Fleas in the day and tigers in the night,
The wild bands struck and fled to strike anew
And drop the curtain of the empty blue
Behind them, passing like the wrath of God.

The failing year had lit the goldenrod
Against the tingling nights, now well begun;
The sunflowers strove to hoard the paling sun
For winter cheer; and leagues of prairie glowed
With summer's dying flare, when fifty rode
From Wallace northward, trailing Roman Nose,
The mad Cheyenne. A motley band were
      those—
Scouts, hunters, captains, colonels, brigadiers;
Wild lads who found adventure in arrears,
And men of beard whom Danger's lure made
      young—
The drift and wreckage of the great war, flung
Along the brawling border. Two and two,
The victor and the vanquished, gray and blue,

Rode out across the Kansas plains together,
Hearts singing to the croon of saddle leather
And jingling spurs. The buffalo, at graze
Like dairy cattle, hardly deigned to raise
Their shaggy heads and watch the horsemen
    pass.
Like bursting case-shot, clumps of blue-joint
    grass
Exploded round them, hurtling grouse and quail
And plover. Wild hens drummed along the trail
At twilight; and the antelope and deer,
Moved more by curiosity than fear,
Went trotting off to pause and gaze their fill.
Past Short Nose and the Beaver, jogging still,
They followed hot upon a trail that shrank
At every tangent draw. Their horses drank
The autumn-lean Republican and crossed;
And there at last the dwindled trail was lost
Where sandhills smoked against a windy sky.

Perplexed and grumbling, disinclined to try
The upper reaches of the stream, they pressed
Behind Forsyth, their leader, pricking west
With Beecher there beside him in the van.
They might have disobeyed a lesser man;
For what availed another wild goose chase,
Foredoomed to end some God-forsaken place
With twilight dying on the prairie rim?
But Fame had blown a trumpet over him;
And men recalled that Shenandoah ride
With Sheridan, the stemming of the tide
Of rabble armies wrecked at Cedar Creek,
When thirty thousand hearts, no longer weak,
Were made one victor's heart.

And so the band
Pushed westward up the lonely river land
Four saddle days from Wallace. Then at last
They came to where another band had passed
With shoeless ponies, following the sun.
Some miles the new trail ran as lean creeks run
In droughty weather; then began to grow.
Here other hoofs had swelled it, there, travaux;
And more and more the circumjacent plains
Had fed the trail, as when torrential rains
Make prodigal the gullies and the sloughs,
And prairie streams, late shrunken to an ooze,
Appal stout swimmers. Scarcity of game
(But yesterday both plentiful and tame)
And recent pony-droppings told a tale
Of close pursuit. All day they kept the trail
And slept upon it in their boots that night
And saddled when the first gray wash of light
Was on the hill tops. Past the North Fork's
    mouth
It led, and, crossing over to the south,
Struck up the valley of the Rickaree—
So broad by now that twenty, knee to knee,
Might ride thereon, nor would a single calk
Bite living sod.

        Proceeding at a walk,
The troopers followed, awed by what they
    dared.
It seemed the low hills stood aloof, nor cared,
Disowning them; that all the gullies mocked
The jingling gear of Folly where it walked
The road to Folly's end. The low day changed
To evening. Did the prairie stare estranged,

The knowing sun make haste to be away?
They saw the fingers of the failing day
Grow longer, groping for the homeward trail.
They saw the sun put on a bloody veil
And disappear.   A flock of crows hurrahed.

Dismounting in the eerie valley, awed
With purple twilight and the evening star,
They camped beside the stream.   A gravel bar
Here split the shank-deep Rickaree in two
And made a little island.   Tall grass grew
Among its scattered alders, and there stood
A solitary sapling cottonwood
Within the lower angle of the sand.

No jesting cheered the saddle-weary band
That night; no fires were kindled to invoke
Tales grim with cannon flare and battle smoke
Remembered, and the glint of slant steel rolled
Up roaring steeps.   They ate short rations cold
And thought about tomorrow and were dumb.

A hint of morning had begun to come;
So faint as yet that half the stars at least
Discredited the gossip of the east.
The grazing horses, blowing at the frost,
Were shadows, and the ghostly sentries tossed
Their arms about them, drowsy in the chill.

Was something moving yonder on the hill
To westward?   It was there—it wasn't there.
Perhaps some wolfish reveller, aware
Of dawn, was making home. 'Twas there again!

And now the bubble world of snoring men
Was shattered, and a dizzy wind, that hurled
Among the swooning ruins of the world
Disintegrating dreams, became a shout:
"Turn out! Turn out! The Indians! Turn
    out!"
Hearts pounding with the momentary funk
Of cold blood spurred to frenzy, reeling drunk
With sleep, men stumbled up and saw the hill
Where shadows of a dream were blowing still—
No—mounted men were howling down the
    slopes!
The horses, straining at their picket ropes,
Reared snorting. Barking carbines flashed and
    gloomed,
Smearing the giddy picture. War drums
    boomed
And shaken rawhide crackled through the din.
A horse that trailed a bounding picket pin
Made off in terror. Others broke and fled.
Then suddenly the silence of the dead
Had fallen, and the slope in front was bare
And morning had become a startled stare
Across the empty prairie, white with frost.

Five horses and a pair of pack mules lost!
That left five donkeys for the packs. Men poked
Sly banter at the mountless ones, invoked
The "infantry" to back them, while they threw
The saddles on and, boot to belly, drew
Groan-fetching cinches tight.

                          A scarlet streak
Was growing in the east. Amid the reek

Of cowchip fires that sizzled with the damp
The smell of coffee spread about the camp
A mood of peace. But 'twas a lying mood;
For suddenly the morning solitude
Was solitude no longer. "Look!" one cried.
The resurrection dawn, as prophesied,
Lacked nothing but the trump to be fulfilled!
They wriggled from the valley grass! They
        spilled
Across the sky rim! North and south and west
Increasing hundreds, men and ponies, pressed
Against the few.

                    'Twas certain death to flee.
The way left open down the Rickaree
To where the valley narrowed to a gap
Was plainly but the baiting of a trap.
Who rode that way would not be riding far.
"Keep cool now, men! Cross over to the bar!"
The colonel shouted. Down they went pell-
        mell,
Churning the creek. A heaven-filling yell
Assailed them. Was it triumph? Was it rage?
Some few wild minutes lengthened to an age
While fumbling fingers stripped the horses'
        backs
And tied the horses. Crouched behind the
        packs
And saddles now, they fell with clawing hands
To digging out and heaping up the sands
Around their bodies. Shots began to fall—
The first few spatters of a thunder squall—
And still the Colonel strolled about the field,
Encouraging the men. A pack mule squealed

And floundered. "Down!" men shouted.
    "Take it cool,"
The Colonel answered; "we can eat a mule
When this day's work is over. Wait the word,
Then see that every cartridge wings a bird.
Don't shoot too fast."

                        The dizzy prairie spun
With painted ponies, weaving on the run
A many colored noose. So dances Death,
Bedizened like a harlot, when the breath
Of Autumn flutes among the shedding boughs
And scarlets caper and the golds carouse
And bronzes trip it and the late green leaps.
And then, as when the howling winter heaps
The strippings of the hickory and oak
And hurls them in a haze of blizzard smoke
Along an open draw, the warriors formed
To eastward down the Rickaree, and stormed
Against the isle, their solid front astride
The shallow water.

                    "Wait!" the Colonel cried;
"Keep cool now!"—Would he never say the
    word?
They heard the falling horses shriek; they heard
The smack of smitten flesh, the whispering
    rush
Of arrows, bullets whipping through the brush
And flicked sand *phutting;* saw the rolling eyes
Of war-mad ponies, crooked battle cries
Lost in the uproar, faces in a blast
Of color, color, and the whirlwind last
Of all dear things forever.

"Now!"

                                    The fear,
The fleet, sick dream of friendly things and
      dear
Dissolved in thunder; and between two breaths
Men sensed the sudden splendor that is Death's,
The wild clairvoyant wonder. Shadows
      screamed
Before the kicking Spencers, split and streamed
About the island in a flame-rent shroud.
And momently, with hoofs that beat the cloud,
Winged with the mad momentum of the charge,
A war horse loomed unnaturally large
Above the burning ring of rifles there,
Lit, sprawling, in the midst and took the air
And vanished. And the storming hoofs roared
      by.
And suddenly the sun, a handbreadth high,
Was peering through the clinging battle-blur.

Along the stream, wherever bushes were
Or clumps of bluejoint, lurking rifles played
Upon the isle—a point-blank enfilade,
Horse-slaughtering and terrible to stand;
And southward there along the rising land
And northward where the valley was a plain,
The horsemen galloped, and a pelting rain
Of arrows fell.

                        Now someone, lying near
Forsyth, was yelling in his neighbor's ear
"They've finished Sandy!" For a giant whip,
It seemed, laid hot along the Colonel's hip

A lash of torture, and his face went gray
And pinched. And voices boomed above the
    fray,
"Is Sandy dead?" So, rising on a knee
That anyone who feared for him might see,
He shouted: "Never mind—it's nothing bad!"
And noting how the wild face of a lad
Yearned up at him—the youngest face of all,
With cheeks like Rambeau apples in the fall,
Eyes old as terror—"Son, you're doing well!"
He cried and smiled; and that one lived to tell
The glory of it in the after days.

Now presently the Colonel strove to raise
The tortured hip to ease it, when a stroke
As of a dull ax bit a shin that broke
Beneath his weight. Dragged backward in a pit,
He sat awhile against the wall of it
And strove to check the whirling of the land.
Then, noticing how some of the command
Pumped lead too fast and threw their shells
    away,
He set about to crawl to where they lay
And tell them. Something whisked away his hat,
And for a green-sick minute after that
The sky rained stars. Then vast ear-hollows
    rang
With brazen noises, and a sullen pang
Was like a fire that smouldered in his skull.
He gazed about him groggily. A lull
Had fallen on the battle, and he saw
How pairs of horsemen galloped down the draw,
Recovering the wounded and the dead.
The snipers on the river banks had fled

To safer berths; but mounted hundreds still
Swarmed yonder on the flat and on the hill,
And long range arrows fell among the men.

The island had become a slaughter pen.
Of all the mules and horses, one alone
Still stood. He wobbled with a gurgling moan,
Legs wide, his drooping muzzle dripping blood;
And some still wallowed in a scarlet mud
And strove to rise, with threshing feet aloft.
But most lay still, as when the spring is soft
And work-teams share the idleness of cows
On Sunday, and a glutted horse may drowse,
Loose-necked, forgetting how the plowshare
        drags.
Bill Wilson yonder lay like bundled rags,
And so did Chalmers. Farley over there,
With one arm limp, was taking special care
To make the other do; it did, no doubt.
And Morton yonder with an eye shot out
Was firing slowly, but his gun barrel shook.
And Mooers, the surgeon, with a sightless look
Of mingled expectation and surprise,
Had got a bullet just above the eyes;
But Death was busy and neglected him.

Now all the while, beneath the low hill rim
To southward, where a sunning slope arose
To look upon the slaughter, Roman Nose
Was sitting, naked of his battle-gear.
In vain his chestnut stallion, tethered near,
Had sniffed the battle, whinnying to go
Where horses cried to horses there below,
And men to men. By now a puzzled word
Ran round the field, and baffled warriors heard,

And out of bloody mouths the dying spat
The question: "Where is Roman Nose, the
    Bat?
While other men are dying, where is he?"
So certain of the mighty rode to see,
And found him yonder sitting in the sun.
They squatted round him silently. And one
Got courage for a voice at length, and said:
"Your people there are dying, and the dead
Are many." But the Harrier of Men
Kept silence. And the bold one, speaking then
To those about him, said: "You see today
The one whom all the warriors would obey,
Whatever he might wish. His heart is faint.
He has not even found the strength to paint
His face, you see!" The Flame of Many Roofs
Still smouldered there. The Midnight Wind
    of Hoofs
Kept mute. "Our brothers, the Arapahoes,"
Another said, "will tell of Roman Nose;
Their squaws will scorn him; and the Sioux
    will say
'He was not like the men we were that day
When all the soldiers died by Peno ford!'"

They saw him wince, as though the words had
    gored
His vitals. Then he spoke. His voice was
    low.
"My medicine is broken. Long ago
One made a bonnet for a mighty man,
My father's father; and the good gift ran
From sire to son, and we were men of might.
For he who wore the bonnet in a fight

Could look on Death, and Death would fear
    him much,
So long as he should let no metal touch
The food he ate. But I have been a fool.
A woman lifted with an iron tool
The bread I ate this morning. What you say
Is good to hear."

                    He cast his robe away,
Got up and took the bonnet from its case
And donned it; put the death-paint on his
    face
And mounted, saying "Now I go to die!"
Thereat he lifted up a bull-lunged cry
That clamored far among the hills around;
And dying men took courage at the sound
And muttered "He is coming."

                            Now it fell
That those upon the island heard a yell
And looked about to see from whence it grew.
They saw a war-horse hurtled from the blue,
A big-boned chestnut, clean and long of limb,
That did not dwarf the warrior striding him,
So big the man was. Naked as the day
The neighbors sought his mother's lodge to say
'This child shall be a trouble to his foes'
(Save for a gorgeous bonnet), Roman Nose
Came singing on the run. And as he came
Mad hundreds hailed him, booming like a
    flame
That rages over slough grass, pony tall.
They formed behind him in a solid wall
And halted at a lifting of his hand.

[93]

The troopers heard him bellow some command.
They saw him wheel and wave his rifle high;
And distant hills were peopled with the cry
He flung at Death, that mighty men of old,
Long dead, might hear the coming of the bold
And know the land still nursed the ancient breed.
Then, followed by a thundering stampede,
He charged the island where the rifles brawled.
And some who galloped nearest him recalled
In after days, what some may choose to doubt,
How suddenly the hubbuboo went out
In silence, and a wild white brilliance broke
About him, and the cloud of battle smoke
Was thronged with faces not of living men.
Then terribly the battle roared again.
And those who tell it saw him reel and sag
Against the stallion, like an empty bag,
Then slip beneath the mill of pony hoofs.

So Roman Nose, the Flame of Many Roofs,
Flared out. And round the island swept the
    foe—
Wrath-howling breakers with an undertow
Of pain that wailed and murmuring dismay.

Now Beecher, with the limp he got that day
At Gettysburg, rose feebly from his place,
Unearthly moon-dawn breaking on his face,
And staggered over to the Colonel's pit.
Half crawling and half falling into it,
"I think I have a fatal wound," he said;
And from his mouth the hard words bubbled red
In witness of the sort of hurt he had.
"No, Beecher, no! It cannot be so bad!"

The other begged, though certain of the end;
For even then the features of the friend
Were getting queer. "Yes, Sandy, yes—
    goodnight,"
The stricken muttered. Whereupon the fight
No longer roared for him; but one who grieved
And fought thereby could hear the rent chest
    heaved
With struggling breath that couldn't leave the
    man.
And by and by the whirling host began
To scatter, most withdrawing out of range.
Astonished at the suddenness of change
From dawn to noon, the troopers saw the sun.

To eastward yonder women had begun
To glean the fallen, wailing as they piled
The broken loves of mother, maid and child
On pony-drags; remembering their wont
Of heaping thus the harvest of the hunt
To fill the kettles these had sat around.

Forsyth now strove to view the battleground,
But could not for the tortured hip and limb;
And so they passed a blanket under him
And four men heaved the corners; then he saw.
"Well, Grover, have they other cards to draw,
Or have they played the pack?" he asked a scout.
And that one took a plug of chewing out
And gnawed awhile, then spat and said:
    "Dunno;
I've fit with Injuns thirty year or so
And never see the like of this till now.
We made a lot of good ones anyhow,
Whatever else—."

Just then it came to pass
Some rifles, hidden yonder in the grass,
Took up the sentence with a snarling rip
That made men duck. One let his corner slip.
The Colonel tumbled, and the splintered shin
Went crooked, and the bone broke through
    the skin;
But what he said his angel didn't write.

'Twas plain the foe had wearied of the fight,
Though scores of wary warriors kept the field
And circled, watching for a head revealed
Above the slaughtered horses. Afternoon
Waned slowly, and a wind began to croon—
Like memory. The sapling cottonwood
Responded with a voice of widowhood.
The melancholy heavens wove a pall.
Night hid the valley. Rain began to fall.

How good is rain when from a sunlit scarp
Of heaven falls a silver titan's harp
For winds to play on, and the new green swirls
Beneath the dancing feet of April girls,
And thunder-claps applaud the meadow lark!
How dear to be remembered—rainy dark
When Youth and Wonder snuggle safe abed
And hear creation bustling overhead
With fitful hushes when the eave *drip-drops*
And everything about the whole house stops
To hear what now the buds and grass may think!

Night swept the island with a brush of ink.
They heard the endless drizzle sigh and pass
And whisper to the bushes and the grass,

*Sh—sh—*for men were dying in the rain;
And there was that low singing that is pain,
And curses muttered lest a stout heart break.

As one who lies with fever half awake
And sets the vague real shepherding a drove
Of errant dreams, the broken Colonel strove
For order in the nightmare. Willing hands
With knife and plate fell digging in the sands
And throwing out a deep surrounding trench.
Graves, yawning briefly in the inky drench,
Were satisfied with something no one saw.
Carved horse meat passed around for wolfing
    raw
And much was cached to save it from the sun.

Now when the work about the camp was done
And all the wounds had got rude handed care,
The Colonel called the men about him there
And spoke of Wallace eighty miles away.
Who started yonder might not see the day;
Yet two must dare that peril with the tale
Of urgent need; and if the two should fail,
God help the rest!

                    It seemed that everyone
Who had an arm left fit to raise a gun
And legs for swinging leather begged to go.
But all agreed with old Pierre Trudeau,
The grizzled trapper, when he ''lowed he
    knowed
The prairie like a farmer did a road,
And many was the Injun he had fooled.'
And Stillwell's youth and daring overruled

The others. Big he was and fleet of limb
And for his laughing pluck men honored him,
Despite that weedy age when boys begin
To get a little conscious of the chin
And jokers dub them "Whiskers" for the lack.
These two were swallowed in the soppy black
And wearily the sodden night dragged by.

At last the chill rain ceased. A dirty sky
Leaked morning. Culver, Farley, Day and
    Smith
Had found a comrade to adventure with
And come upon the country that is kind.
But Mooers was slow in making up his mind
To venture, though with any breath he might.
Stark to the drab indecency of light,
The tumbled heaps, that once were horses, lay
With naked ribs and haunches lopped away—
Good friends at need with all their fleetness
    gone.
Like wolves that smell a feast the foe came on,
A skulking pack. They met a gust of lead
That flung them with their wounded and their
    dead
Back to the spying summits of the hills,
Content to let the enemy that kills
Without a wound complete the task begun.

Dawn cleared the sky, and all day long the sun
Shone hotly through a lens of amethyst—
Like some incorrigible optimist
Who overworks the sympathetic rôle.
All day the troopers sweltered in the bowl
Of soppy sand, and wondered if the two
Were dead by now; or had they gotten through?

And if they hadn't—What about the meat?
Another day or two of steaming heat
Would fix it for the buzzards and the crows;
And there'd be choicer banqueting for those
If no one came.
                        So when a western hill
Burned red and blackened, and the stars came
          chill,
Two others started crawling down the flat
For Wallace; and for long hours after that
Men listened, listened, listened for a cry,
But heard no sound. And just before the sky
Began to pale, the two stole back unhurt.
The dark was full of shadow men, alert
To block the way wherever one might go.

Alas, what chance for Stillwell and Trudeau?
That day the dozen wounded bore their plight
Less cheerfully than when the rainy night
Had held so great a promise. All day long,
As one who hums a half forgotten song
By poignant bits, the dying surgeon moaned;
But when the west was getting sober-toned,
He choked a little and forgot the tune.
And men were silent, wondering how soon
They'd be like that.
                        Now when the tipping Wain,
Above the Star, poured slumber on the plain,
Jack Donovan and Pliley disappeared
Down river where the starry haze made weird
The narrow gulch. They seemed as good as
          dead;
And all next day the parting words they said,
"We won't be coming back," were taken wrong.

The fourth sun since the battle lingered long.
Putrescent horseflesh now befouled the air.
Some tried to think they liked the prickly pear.
Some tightened up their belts a hole or so.
And certain of the wounded babbled low
Of places other than the noisome pits,
Because the fever sped their straying wits
Like homing bumblebees that know the hive.
That day the Colonel found his leg alive
With life that wasn't his.

                   The fifth sun crept;
The evening dawdled; morning overslept.
It seemed the dark would never go away;
The kiotes filled it with a roundelay
Of toothsome horses smelling to the sky.

But somehow morning happened by and by.
All day the Colonel scanned the prairie rims
And found it hard to keep away the whims
That dogged him; often, wide awake, he
    dreamed.
The more he thought of it, the more it seemed
That all should die of hunger wasn't fair;
And so he called the sound men round him there
And spoke of Wallace and the chance they
    stood
To make their way to safety, if they would.
As for himself and other cripples—well,
They'd take a chance, and if the worst befell,
Were soldiers.

             There was silence for a space
While each man slyly sought his neighbor's face

To see what better thing a hope might kill.
Then there was one who growled: "The hell
    we will!
We've fought together and we'll die so too!"
One might have thought relief had come in
    view
To hear the shout that rose.

                   The slow sun sank.
The empty prairie gloomed. The horses stank.
The kiotes sang. The starry dark was cold.

That night the prowling wolves grew over bold
And one was cooking when the sun came up.
It gave the sick a little broth to sup;
And for the rest, they joked and made it do.
And all day long the cruising buzzards flew
Above the island, eager to descend;
While, raucously prophetic of the end,
The crows wheeled round it hungrily to pry;
And mounted warriors loomed against the sky
To peer and vanish. Darkness fell at last;
But when the daylight came and when it
    passed
The Colonel scarcely knew, for things got
    mixed;
The moment was forever, strangely fixed,
And never in a moment. Still he kept
One certain purpose, even when he slept,
To cheer the men by seeming undismayed.
But when the eighth dawn came, he grew
    afraid
Of his own weakness. Stubbornly he sat,
His tortured face half hidden by his hat,

And feigned to read a novel one had found
Among the baggage.   But the print went
    round
And wouldn't talk however it was turned.

At last the morning of the ninth day burned.
Again he strove to regiment the herds
Of dancing letters into marching words,
When suddenly the whole command went mad.
They yelled; they danced the way the letters
    had;
They tossed their hats.

                    Then presently he knew
'Twas cavalry that made the hillside blue—
The cavalry from Wallace!

VIII. THE YELLOW GOD

Autumn's goad
Had thronged the weed-grown Powder River
    Road
With bison following the shrinking green.
Again the Platte and Smoky Hill had seen
The myriads nosing at the dusty hem
Of Summer's robe; and, drifting after them,
The wild marauders vanished. Winter came;
And lo! the homesteads echoed with a name
That was a ballad sung, a saga told;
For, once men heard it, somehow it was
    old
With Time's rich hoarding and the bardic
    lyres.
By night the settlers hugged their cowchip
    fires
And talked of Custer, while the children
    heard
The way the wild wind dramatized the word
With men and horses roaring to the fight
And valiant bugles crying down the night,
Far-blown from Cedar Creek or Fisher's Hill.
And in their sleep they saw him riding still,
A part of all things wonderful and past,
His bright hair streaming in the battle blast
Above a surf of sabres! Roofs of shale
And soddy walls seemed safer for the tale,
The prairie kinder for that name of awe.
For now the Battle of the Washita

Was fought at every hearthstone in the land.
'Twas song to talk of Custer and his band:
The blizzard dawn, the march from Camp
    Supply,
Blind daring with the compass for an eye
To pierce the writhing haze; the icy fords,
The freezing sleeps; the finding of the hordes
That deemed the bitter weather and the snows
Their safety—Kiowas, Arapahoes,
Cheyennes, Comanches—miles of river flat
One village; Custer crouching like a cat
Among the drifts; the numbing lapse of night;
The brass band blaring in the first wan light,
The cheers, the neighing, and the wild swoop
    down
To widow-making in a panic town
Of widow-makers! O 'twas song to say
How Old Black Kettle paid his life that day
For bloody dawns of terror! Lyric words
Dwelt long upon his slaughtered pony herds,
His lodges burning for the roofs that blazed
That dreadful year! Rejoicing Kansas raised
Her eyes beyond the days of her defeat
And saw her hills made mighty with the wheat,
The tasselled corn ranks marching on the
    plain;
The wonder-working of the sun and rain
And faith and labor; plenty out of dearth;
Man's mystic marriage with the virgin Earth,
A hard-won bride.

        And April came anew;
But there were those—and they were human
    too—

For whom the memory of other springs
Sought vainly in the growing dusk of things
The ancient joy. Along the Smoky Hill
The might they could no longer hope to kill
Brawled west again, where maniacs of toil
Were chaining down the violated soil,
And plows went wiving in the bison range,
An alien-childed mother growing strange
With younger loves. May deepened in the
    sloughs
When down the prairie swept the wonder
    news
Of what had happened at the Great Salt Lake,
And how, at last, the crawling iron snake
Along the Platte had lengthened to the sea.
So shadows of a thing that was to be
Grew darker in the land.

                        Four years went by,
And still the solemn music of a lie
Kept peace in all the country of the Sioux.
Unharried yonder, still the bison knew
The meadows of Absoraka and throve;
But now no more the Hoary Herdsman drove
His countless cattle past the great Platte road.
Still honoring the treaty, water flowed,
And grass grew, faithful to the plighted word.
Then yonder on the Yellowstone was heard
The clank of sabers; and the red men saw
How Long Hair, still the Wolf of Washita,
Went spying with his pack along the stream,
While others, bitten with a crazy dream,
Were driving stakes and peeping up the flat.
Just so it was that summer on the Platte

Before the evil came. And devil boats
Came up with stinking thunder in their throats
To scare the elk and make the bison shy.
So there was fighting yonder where the lie
Was singing flat; though nothing came of it.

And once again the stunted oaks were lit,
And down across the prairie howled the cold;
And spring came back, exactly as of old,
To resurrect the waters and the grass.
The summer deepened peacefully—alas,
The last of happy summers, cherished long
As Sorrow hoards the wreckage of a song
Whose wounding lilt is dearer for the wound.
The children laughed; contented mothers
      crooned
About their lodges. Nothing was afraid.
The warriors talked of hunting, in the shade,
Or romped with crowing babies on their
      backs.
The meat was plenty on the drying racks;
The luscious valleys made the ponies glad;
And travellers knew nothing that was bad
To tell of any village they had known.
No white men yonder on the Yellowstone,
Nor any sign of trouble anywhere!

Then once again the Wolf with yellow hair
Was on the prowl; for Summer turning
      brown,
Beheld him lead his men and wagons down
To pierce the Hills where Inyan Kara towers,
Brawl southward through that paradise of
      flowers

And singing streams and pines to French's
    Creek:
Beheld him even climbing Harney Peak
To spy the land, as who should say him no!
Had grasses failed? Had water ceased to flow?
Were pledges wind?

            Now scarce the sloughs were sere
When Custer, crying in the wide world's ear
What every need and greed could understand,
Made all men see the Black Hills wonderland
Where Fortune waited, ready with a bow.
What fertile valleys pining for the plow!
What lofty forests given to the birds,
What luscious cattle pastures to the herds
Of elk and deer! What flower-enchanted parks,
Now lonely with the quails and meadowlarks,
Awaited men beneath the shielding peaks!
And in the creeks—in all the crystal creeks—
The blessèd creeks—O wonder to behold!—
Free gold—the god of rabbles—holy gold—
And gold in plenty from the grass-roots down!

The Black Hills Country! Heard in every town,
That incantation of a wizard horn
Wrought madness. Farmers caught it in the
    corn
To shuck no more. No glory of the sward
Outdazzled yonder epiphanic Lord—
The only revelation that was sure!
And through the cities went the singing lure,
Where drearily the human welter squirms
Like worms that lick the slime of other worms
That all may flourish. Squalor saw the gleam,
And paupers mounted in a splendid dream

The backs of luckless men, for now the weak
Inherited the earth! The fat, the sleek
Envisaged that apocalypse, and saw
Obesity to put the cringe of awe
In knees of leanness!

                  Sell the family cow!
Go pawn the homestead! Life was knocking
     now!
There might not ever be another knock.
Bring forth the hoarding of the hidden sock,
Poor coppers from the dear dead eyes of Joy!
Go seek the god that weighs the soul by troy;
Be saved, and let the devil take the rest!
The West—the golden West—the siren West—
Behold the rainbow's end among her peaks!
For in the creeks—in all the crystal creeks—
The blessèd creeks—!

               So wrought the rueful dream.
Chinooks of hope fed full the human stream,
Brief thawings of perennial despair.
And steadily the man-flood deepened there
With every moon along the Sioux frontier,
Where still the treaty held—a rotten wier
Already trickling with a leak of men.
And some of those came drifting back again,
Transfigured palmers from the Holy Lands,
With true salvation gleaming in their hands
Now cleansed of labor. Thus the wonder grew.

And there were flinty hearts among the Sioux
That fall and winter. Childish, heathen folk,
Their god was but a spirit to invoke

Among the hushes of a lonely hill;
An awfulness when winter nights were still;
A mystery, a yearning to be felt
When birds returned and snow began to melt
And miracles were doing in the grass.
Negotiable Divinity, alas,
They had not yet the saving grace to know!

Nor did the hard hearts soften with the snow,
When from the high gray wilderness of rain
Johannine voices of the goose and crane
Foretold the Coming to a world enthralled;
For still along the teeming border brawled
The ever growing menace.

                    Summer bloomed;
But many, with the prescience of the doomed,
Could feel the shaping of the end of things
In all that gladness. How the robin sings
The sweeter in the ghastly calm that aches
With beauty lost, before the cyclone breaks!
And helpless watchers feel it as a pang,
Because of all the times the robin sang
Scarce noted in the melody of then.
About the lodges gray and toothless men
Bemoaned the larger time when life was good.
Hey-hey, what warriors then, what hardihood!
What terror of the Sioux among their foes!
What giants, gone, alas, these many snows—
And they who knew so near their taking off!
Now beggars at the Great White Father's trough
Forgot the bow and waited to be swilled.
The woman-hearted god the White Man killed
Bewitched the people more with every moon.
The buffalo would join the fathers soon.

The world was withered like a man grown old.
A few more grasses, and the Sioux would hold
A little paper, dirtied with a lie,
For all that used to be.   Twas time to die.
Hey-hey, the braver days when life was new!

But there were strong hearts yet among the
    Sioux
Despite the mumbling of the withered gums.
That summer young men chanted to the drums
Of mighty deeds; and many went that fall
Where Crazy Horse and Sitting Bull and Gall
Were shepherding their people on the Tongue
And Powder yet, as when the world was young,
Contemptuous of alien ways and gods.

Now when the candles of the goldenrods
Were guttering about the summer's bier,
And unforgetting days were hushed to hear
Some rumor of a lone belated bird,
It came to pass the Great White Father's word
Assembled many on the White to meet
The Long Knife chieftains.   Bitter words and
    sweet
Grew rankly there; and stubbornly the wills
Of children met the hagglers for the Hills,
The lust for gold begetting lust for gold.
The young moon grew and withered and was
    old,
And still the latest word was like the first.

Then talking ended and the man-dam burst
To loose the living flood upon the West.
All winter long it deepened, and the crest

Came booming with the February thaw.
The torrent setting in through Omaha
Ground many a grist of greed, and loud
    Cheyenne
Became a tail-race running mules and men
Hell-bent for Eldorado. Yankton vied
With Sidney in the combing of the tide
For costly wreckage. Giddily it swirled
Where Custer City shouted to the world
And Deadwood was a howl, and Nigger Hill
A cry from Pisgah. Unabated still,
Innumerable distant freshets flowed.
The bison trail became a rutted road
And prairie schooners cruised the rolling
    Spring.
In labor with a monstrous farrowing,
The river packets grunted; and the plains
Were startled at the spawning of the trains
Along the Platte.

       So, bitten by the imp
Of much-for-nought, the gambler and the
    pimp,
The hero and the coward and the fool,
The pious reader of the golden rule
By decimals, the dandy and the gawk,
The human eagle and the wingless hawk
Alert for prey, the graybeard and the lad,
The murderer, the errant Galahad,
Mistaken in the color of the gleam—
All dreamers of the old pathetic dream—
Pursued what no pursuing overtakes.

IX. THE VILLAGE OF CRAZY HORSE

Meanwhile among the Powder River breaks,
Where cottonwoods and plums and stunted
    oaks
Made snug his village of a hundred smokes,
Young Crazy Horse was waiting for the spring.
Well found his people were in everything
That makes a winter good. But more than
    food
And shelter from the hostile solitude
Sustained them yonder when the sun fled far
And rustling ghost-lights capered round the
    Star
And moons were icy and the blue snow whined;
Or when for days the world went blizzard blind
And devils of the North came howling down.
For something holy moved about the town
With Crazy Horse.

                    No chieftainship had run,
Long cherished in the blood of sire and son,
To clothe him with the might he wielded then.
The Ogalalas boasted taller men
But few of fairer body. One might look
And think of water running in a brook
Or maybe of a slender hickory tree;
And something in his face might make one see
A flinty shaft-head very keen to go,
Because a hero's hand is on the bow,

His eye upon the mark. But nothing seen
About his goodly making or his mien
Explained the man; and other men were bold.
Unnumbered were the stories that were told
(And still the legend glorified the truth)
About his war-fond, pony-taming youth
When Hump the Elder was a man to fear;
And where one went, the other would be near,
For there was love between the man and lad.
And it was good to tell what fights they had
With roving bands of Utes or Snakes or Crows.
And now that Hump was gone these many snows,
His prowess lingered. So the legend ran.
But neither Hump nor any other man
Could give the gift that was a riddle still.
What lonely vigils on a starry hill,
What fasting in the time when boyhood dies
Had put the distant seeing in his eyes,
The power in his silence? What had taught
That getting is a game that profits naught
And giving is a high heroic deed?
His plenty never neighbored with a need
Among his band. A good tough horse to ride,
The gear of war, and some great dream inside
Were Crazy Horse's wealth. It seemed the dim
And larger past had wandered back in him
To shield his people in the days of wrong.
His thirty years were like a brave old song
That men remember and the women croon
To make their babies brave.

               Now when the moon
Had wearied of December and was gone,
And bitterly the blizzard time came on,

The Great White Father had a word to say.
The frost-bit runners rode a weary way
To bring the word, and this is what it said:
"All bands, before another moon is dead,
Must gather at the agencies or share
The fate of hostiles." Grandly unaware
Of aught but its own majesty and awe,
The big word blustered. Yet the people saw
The snow-sift snaking in the grasses, heard
The Northwind bellow louder than the word
To make them shudder with the winter fear.
"You see that there are many children here,"
Said Crazy Horse. "Our herd is getting lean.
We can not go until the grass is green.
It is a very foolish thing you say."
And so the surly runners rode away
And Crazy Horse's people stayed at home.

And often were the days a howling gloam
Between two howling darks; nor could one tell
When morning broke and when the long night
    fell;
For 'twas a winter such as old men cite
To overawe and set the youngsters right
With proper veneration for the old.
The ponies huddled humpbacked in the cold
And, dog-like, gnawed the bark of cottonwood.
But where the cuddled rawhide lodges stood
Men laughed and yarned and let the blizzard
    roar,
Unwitting how the tale the runners bore
Prepared the day of sorrow.

                    March boomed in,
And still the people revelled in their sin

Nor thought of woe already on the way.
Then, when the night was longer than the day
By just about an old man's wink and nod,
As sudden as the storied wrath of God,
And scarce more human, retribution came.

The moony wind that night was like a flame
To sear whatever naked flesh it kissed.
The dry snow powder coiled and struck and
    hissed
Among the lodges. Haloes mocked the moon.
The boldest tale was given over soon
For kinder evenings; and the dogs were still
Before the prowling foe no pack might kill,
The subtle fang that feared not any fang.
But ever nearer, nearer, shod hoofs rang
To southward, unsuspected in the town.
Three cavalry battalions, flowing down
The rugged canyon bed of Otter Creek
With Reynolds, clattered out across the bleak
High prairie, eerie in the fitful light,
Where ghostly squadrons howled along the
    night,
Their stinging sabers gleaming in the wind.
All night they sought the village that had sinned
Yet slept the sleep of virtue, unafraid.
The Bear swung round; the stars began to
    fade;
The low moon stared. Then, floating in the
    puffs
Of wind-whipped snow, the Powder River bluffs
Gloomed yonder, and the scouts came back to
    tell
Of many sleeping lodges.

Now it fell
That when the bluffs were paling with the glow
Of dawn, and still the tepee tops below
Stood smokeless in the stupor of a dream,
A Sioux boy, strolling down the frozen stream
To find his ponies, wondered at the sound
Of many hoofs upon the frozen ground,
The swishing of the brush. He paused to think.
The herd, no doubt, was coming for a drink;
He'd have to chop a hole. And while he stood,
The spell of dawn upon him, from the wood—
How queer!—they issued marching four by four
As though enchanted, breasts and muzzles hoar
With frozen breath! Were all the ponies dead,
And these their taller spirits?

      —Then he fled,
The frightened trees and bushes flowing dim,
The blanching bluff tops flinging back at him
His many-echoed yell. A frowsy squaw
Thrust up a lodge flap, blinked about her—saw
What ailed her boy, and fell to screaming shrill.
The startled wolf-dogs, eager for a kill,
Rushed yelping from the lodges. Snapping
  sharp,
As 'twere a short string parting in a harp,
A frosty rifle sounded. Tepees spilled
A half clad rabble, and the valley filled
With uproar, spurting into jets of pain;
For now there swept a gust of killing rain
From where the plunging horses in a cloud
Of powder smoke bore down upon the crowd
To set it scrambling wildly for the breaks.
The waddling grandmas lost their precious aches

In terror for the young they dragged and drove;
Hysteric mothers staggered as they strove
To pack the creepers and the toddlers too;
And grandpas, not forgetting they were Sioux,
Made shift to do a little with the bows,
While stubbornly the young men after those
Retreated fighting through the lead-swept town
And up the sounding steeps.

                              There, looking down
Along the track of terror splotched with red
And dotted with the wounded and the dead,
They saw the blue-coats rage among their roofs,
Their homes flung down and given to the hoofs
Of desecrating wrath. And while they gazed
In helpless grief and fury, torches blazed
And tepees kindled. Casks of powder, stored
Against a doubtful future, belched and roared.
The hurtled lodge poles showered in the gloom,
And rawhide tops, like glutted bats of doom,
Sailed tumbling in the dusk of that despair.

Not long the routed warriors cowered there
Among the rocks and gullies of the steep.
The weakness of a panic-broken sleep
Wore off. Their babies whimpered in the frost.
Their herd was captured. Everything seemed
      lost
But life alone. It made them strong to die.
The death-song, stabbed with many a battle cry,
Blew down the flat—a blizzard of a sound—
And all the rocks and draws and brush around
Spat smoke and arrows in a closing ring.
There fell a sudden end of plundering.

Abruptly as they came the raiders fled,
And certain of their wounded, men have said,
Were left to learn what hells are made of wrath.

Now, gleaning in that strewn tornado path
Their dead and dying, came the mourning folk
To find a heap for home, a stinking smoke
For plenty. Senseless to the whirling snow,
About the bitter honey of their woe
They swarmed and moaned. What evil had
        they done?
Dear eyes, forever empty of the sun,
Stared up at them. These little faces, old
With pain, and pinched with more than winter
        cold—
Why should they never seek the breast again?
A keening such as wakes the wolf in men
Outwailed the wind. Yet many a thrifty wife,
Long used to serve the urgencies of life
That make death seem a laggard's impudence,
Descended in a rage of commonsense
Upon the wreck, collecting what would do
To fend the cold.

                    Now while the village grew,
A miracle of patches, jerry-built,
The young men, hot upon the trail of guilt
With Crazy Horse, found many a huddled stray
Forlorn along the thousand-footed way
The stolen herd had gone. And all day long
Their fury warmed them and their hearts were
        strong
To meet with any death a man might die;
For still they heard the wounded children cry,

The mourning of the women for the dead.
Nor did they deem that any hero led
The raiders. Surely nothing but the greed
Of terror could devour at such a speed
That pony-laming wallow, drift on drift.

The blue dusk mingled with the driven sift,
And still it seemed the trail of headlong flight
Was making for the wilderness of night
And safety. Then, a little way below
The mouth of Lodge Pole Creek, a dancing
     glow
Went up the bluff. Some few crept close to
     see,
And what they saw was listless misery
That crouched and shivered in a smudge of
     sage.
How well they cooled their baby-killing rage,
Those tentless men without a bite to eat!
And many, rubbing snow upon their feet,
Made faces that were better to behold
Than how their shaking horses took the cold
With tight-tailed rumps against the bitter
     flaw.
Beyond the camp and scattered up the draw
The hungry ponies pawed the frozen ground,
And there was no one anywhere around
To guard them. White-man medicine was
     weak.

Now all the young men, hearing, burned to
     wreak
Their hate upon the foe. A wiser will
Restrained them. "Wait a better time to kill,"

Said Crazy Horse. "Our lives are few to give
And theirs are many. Can our people live
Without the herd? We must not die today.
The time will come when I will lead the way
Where many die."

              Like hungry wolves that prowl
The melancholy marches of the owl
Where cows and calves are grazing unafraid,
The pony stalkers went. A stallion neighed,
Ears pricked to question what the dusk might
        bring;
Then all the others fell to whinnying
And yonder in the camp the soldiers heard.
Some rose to point where many shadows,
        blurred
With driven snow and twilight, topped a rise
And vanished in the smother. Jeering cries
Came struggling back and perished in the
        bruit
Of charging wind. No bugles of pursuit
Aroused the camp. Night howled along the
        slough.

X. THE SUN DANCE

Now wheresoever thawing breezes blew
And green began to prickle in the brown,
There went the tale of Crazy Horse's town
To swell a mood already growing there.
For something more than Spring was in the
    air,
And, mightier than any maiden's eyes,
The Lilith-lure of Perilous Emprise
Was setting all the young men's blood astir.
How fair the more than woman face of her
Whose smile has gulfed how many a daring
    prow!
What cities burn for jewels on her brow;
Upon her lips what vintages are red!
Her lovers are the tallest of the dead
Forever. When the streams of Troas rolled
So many heroes seaward, she was old;
Yet she is young forever to the young.

'Twas now the murmur of the man-flood, flung
Upon the Hills, grew ominously loud.
The whole white world seemed lifted in a
    cloud
To sweep the prairie with a monstrous rain.
Slay one, and there were fifty to be slain!
Give fifty to the flame for torturing,
Then count the marching multitude of Spring
Green blade by blade!

Still wilder rumors grew;
They told of soldiers massed against the Sioux
And waiting till the grass was good, to fall
On Crazy Horse and Sitting Bull and Gall
That all the country might be safe for theft,
And nothing of a warrior race be left
But whining beggars in a feeding pen.
Alas, the rights of men—of other men—
That centenary season of the Free!
No doubt the situation wanted tea
To make it clear! But long before the green
Had topped the hills, the agencies grew lean
Of youth and courage. Did a watch dog bark
Midway between the owl and meadowlark?—
Then other lads with bow and shield and
    lance
Were making for the Region of Romance
Where Sitting Bull's weird medicine was strong
And Crazy Horse's name was like a song
A happy warrior sings before he dies,
And Gall's a wind of many battle cries
That flings a thousand ponies on the doomed.

So where the Powder and the Rosebud boomed,
Men met as water of the melting snows.
The North Cheyennes and North Arapahoes,
Become one people in a common cause
With Brulês, Minneconjoux, Hunkpapas,
Sans Arcs and Ogalalas, came to throng
The valleys; and the villages were long
With camp on camp. Nor was there any
    bluff,
In all the country, that was tall enough
To number half the ponies at a look.

Here young June came with many tales of
    Crook,
The Gray Fox, marching up the Bozeman Road.
How long a dust above his horsemen flowed!
How long a dust his walking soldiers made!
What screaming thunder when the pack-mules
    brayed
And all the six-mule wagon teams replied!
The popping of the whips on sweaty hide,
How like a battle when the foe is bold!
And from the North still other tales were told
By those who heard the steamboats wheeze
    and groan
With stuffs of war along the Yellowstone
To feed the camps already waiting there.
Awaiting what? The might of Yellow Hair
Now coming from the Heart's mouth! Rumor
    guessed
How many Snakes were riding from the West
To join the Whites against their ancient foes;
How many Rees, how many of the Crows
Remembered to be jealous of the Sioux.
Look north, look south—the cloud of trouble
    grew.
Look east, look west—the whole horizon
    frowned.
But it was better to be ringed around
With enemies, to battle and to fail,
Than be a beggar chief like Spotted Tail,
However fattened by a hated hand.

Now when the full moon flooded all the land
Before the laughter of the owls began,
They turned to One who, mightier than Man,

Could help them most—the Spirit in the sun;
For whatsoever wonder-work is done
Upon the needy earth, he does it all.
For him the whole world sickens in the fall
When streams cease singing and the skies go
    gray
And trees and bushes weep their leaves away
In hopeless hushes empty of the bird,
And all day long and all night long are heard
The high geese wailing after their desire.
But, even so, his saving gift of fire
Is given unto miserable men
Until they see him face to face again
And all his magic happen, none knows how.
It was the time when he is strongest now;
And so a holy man whose heart was good
Went forth to find the sacred cottonwood
Belovéd of the Spirit. Straight and high,
A thing of worship yearning for the sky,
It flourished, sunning in a lonely draw;
And there none heard the holy man nor saw
What rites were done, save only one who
    knows
From whence the new moon comes and whither
    goes
The old, and what the stars do all day long.
Thereafter came the people with a song,
The men, the boys, the mothers and the
    maids,
All posy-crowns and blossom-woven braids,
As though a blooming meadow came to see.
And fruitful women danced about the tree
To make the Spirit glad; for, having known
The laughter of the children of their own,

Some goodness of the earth, the giving one,
Was in them and was pleasing to the Sun,
The prairie-loving nourisher of seed.

A warrior who had done the bravest deed
Yet dared that year by any of the Sioux
Now struck the trunk as one who counts a *coup*
Upon a dreaded foe; and prairie gifts
He gave among the poor, for nothing lifts
The heart like giving. Let the coward save—
Big hoard and little heart; but still the brave
Have more with nothing! Singing virgins came
Whose eyes had never learned to droop with
        shame,
Nor was there any present, man or youth,
Could say them aught of ill and say the truth,
For sweet as water in a snow-born brook
Where many birches come and lean to look
Along a mountain gorge, their spirits were.
And each one took the ax they gave to her
And smote the tree with many a lusty stroke;
And with a groan the sleeper in it 'woke
And far hills heard the falling shout of him.
Still rang the axes, cleaving twig and limb
Along the tapered beauty of the bole,
Till, naked to the light, the sacred pole
Lay waiting for the bearers.

                    They who bore
Were chieftains, and their fathers were before,
And all of them had fasted, as they should;
Yet none dared touch the consecrated wood
With naked fingers, out of pious fear.
And once for every season of the year

They paused along the way, remembering
With thanks alike the autumn and the spring,
The winter and the summer.

                          Then it fell
That many warriors, lifting up a yell
That set their ponies plunging, thundered down
Across the center of the circled town
Where presently the holy tree should stand;
For whosoever first of all the band
Could strike the sacred spot with bow or spear
Might gallop deep among the dead that year
Yet be of those whom busy Death forgot.
And sweaty battle raged about the spot
Where screaming ponies, rearing to the thrust
Of screaming ponies, clashed amid the dust,
And riders wrestled in the hoof-made gloam.

So, having safely brought the sun-tree home,
The people feasted as for victory.

And on the second day they dressed the tree
And planted it with sacred songs and vows,
And round it reared a wall of woven boughs
That opened to the mystic source of day.
And with the next dawn mothers came to lay
Their babies down before the holy one,
Each coveting a hero for a son
Or sturdy daughters fit to nurse the bold.
Then when the fourth dawn came the war
         drums rolled;
And from their lodges, lean and rendered pure
With meatless days, those vowing to endure
The death-in-torture to be born again,
Came naked there before the holy men

Who painted them with consecrated paint.
And if a knee seemed loosened, it was faint
With fast and weary vigil, not with dread;
For lo! the multitudinary dead
Pressed round to see if heroes such as they
Still walked the earth despite the smaller day
When 'twas not half so easy to be brave.
Now, prone beneath the pole, as in a grave,
Without a wince each vower took the blade
In chest or back, and through the wound it
    made
Endured the passing of the rawhide thong,
Swung from the pole's top; raised a battle song
To daunt his anguish; staggered to his feet
And, leaning, capered to the war drum's beat
A dizzy rigadoon with Agony.

So all day long the spirit-haunted tree
Bore bloody fruitage, groaning to the strain,
For with the dropping of the ripe-in-pain,
Upon the stem the green-in-courage grew.
And seldom had there fallen on the Sioux
So great a wind of ghostly might as then.
Boys tripped it, bleeding, with the tortured
    men.
The mothers, daughters, sisters, sweethearts,
    wives
Of those who suffered, gashed their flesh with
    knives
To share a little of the loved one's pang;
And all day long the sunning valley rang
With songs of courage; and the mother sod
Received the red libation; and the god
Gave power to his people.

XI. THE SEVENTH MARCHES

                              Far away,
One foggy morning in the midst of May,
Fort Lincoln had beheld the marshalling
Of Terry's forces; heard the bugle sing,
The blaring of the band, the brave hurrah
Of Custer's men recalling Washita
And confident of yet another soon.
How gallantly in column of platoon
(So many doomed and given to the ghost)
Before the weeping women of the post
They sat their dancing horses on parade!
What made the silence suddenly afraid
When, with a brazen crash, the band went
      whist
And, dimmer in the clinging river mist,
The line swung westward? Did the Ree squaws
      know,
Through some wise terror of the ancient
      foe,
To what unearthly land their warriors led
The squadrons? Better suited to the dead
Than to the quick, their chanting of farewell
Grew eerie in the shadow, rose and fell—
The long-drawn yammer of a lonely dog.
But when at length the sun broke through the
      fog,
What reassurance in the wide blue air,
The solid hills, and Custer riding there

With all the famous Seventh at his heel!
And back of those the glint of flowing steel
Above the dusty infantry; the sun's
Young glimmer on the trundled Gatling guns;
And then the mounted Rees; and after that
The loaded pack mules straggling up the flat
And wagons crowding wagons for a mile!

What premonition of the afterwhile
Could darken eyes that saw such glory pass
When, lilting in a muffled blare of brass
Off yonder near the sundering prairie rim,
The Girl I Left Behind Me floated dim
As from the unrecoverable years?
And was it nothing but a freak of tears,
The vision that the grieving women saw?
For suddenly a shimmering veil of awe
Caught up the van. One could have counted ten
While Custer and the half of Custer's men
Were riding up a shining steep of sky
As though to join the dead that do not die
But haunt some storied heaven of the bold.
And then it seemed a smoke of battle rolled
Across the picture, leaving empty air
Above the line that slowly shortened there
And dropped below the prairie and was gone.

Now day by day the column straggled on
While moody May was dribbling out in rain
To make a wagon-wallow of the plain
Between the Muddy and the upper Heart
Where lifeless hills, as by demonic art,
Were hewn to forms of wonderment and fear,
Excited echoes flocked about to hear,

And any sound brought riotous applause,
So long among the scarps and tangled draws
Had clung that silence and the spell of it.
Some fiend-deserted city of the Pit
The region seemed, with crumbling domes and
    spires;
For still it smoked with reminiscent fires,
And in the midst, as 'twere the stream of woe,
A dark flood ran.

                June blustered in with snow,
And all the seasons happened in a week.
Beyond the Beaver and O'Fallon creek
They toiled. Amid the wilderness of breaks
The drainage of the lower Powder makes,
They found a way and brought the wagons
    through;
Nor had they sight or sign of any Sioux
In all that land. Here Reno headed south
With packs and half the troopers for the mouth
Of Mispah, thence to scout the country west
About the Tongue; while Terry and the rest
Pushed onward to the Yellowstone to bide
With Gibbon's men the news of Reno's ride.

Mid June drew on. Slow days of waiting bred
Unhappy rumors. Everybody said
What no one, closely questioned, seemed to
    know.
Enormous numerations of the foe,
By tentative narration made exact
And tagged with all the circumstance of fact,
Discredited the neat official tale.
'Twas well when dawn came burning down
    the vale

And river fogs were lifting like a smoke
And bugles, singing reveille, awoke
A thousand-throated clamor in the herd.
But when the hush was like a warning word
And taps had yielded darkness to the owl,
A horse's whinny or a kiote's howl
Made true the wildest rumors of the noon.

So passed the fateful seventeenth of June
When none might guess how much the gossip
    lacked
To match the unimaginative fact
Of what the upper Rosebud saw that day:
How Crook, with Reno forty miles away,
Had met the hordes of Crazy Horse and Gall,
And all the draws belched cavalries, and all
The ridges bellowed and the river fen
Went dizzy with the press of mounted men—
A slant cyclonic tangle; how the dark
Came not a whit too early, and the lark
Beheld the Gray Fox slinking back amazed
To Goose Creek; what a dust the victors
    raised
Among the Chetish Hills that saw them pass
Triumphant down upon the Greasy Grass
To swell a league-long village. What a road
Their myriad ponies made to that abode
Where live the Tallest of the Shining Past!

Now came the end of waiting, for at last
The scouting squadrons, jogging from the south,
Had joined their comrades at the Rosebud's
    mouth

With doubtful news. That evening by the fires,
According to their dreads or their desires,
The men discussed the story that was told
About a trail, not over three weeks old,
That led across the country from the Tongue,
Struck up the Rosebud forty miles and swung
Again to westward over the divide.
Some said, "We'll find blue sky the other side,
Then back to Lincoln soon!" But more
        agreed
'Twould not be so with Custer in the lead.
"He'll eat his horses when the hardtack's
        gone
Till every man's afoot!" And thereupon
Scarred veterans remembered other days
With Custer—thirsty marches in the blaze
Of Texas suns, with stringy mule to chew;
And times when splinters of the North Pole
        blew
Across the lofty Colorado plains;
And muddy going in the sullen rains
Of Kansas springs, when verily you felt
Your backbone rub the buckle of your belt
Because there weren't any mules to spare.
Aye, there were tales to make the rookies stare
Of Custer's daring and of Custer's luck.
And some recalled that night before they struck
Black Kettle's village. Whew! And what a
        night!
A foot of snow, and not a pipe alight,
And not a fire! You didn't dare to doze,
But kept your fingers on your horse's nose
For fear he'd nicker and the chance be lost.
And all night long there, starry in the frost,

You'd see the steaming Colonel striding by.
And when the first light broke along the sky,
Yet not enough to make a saber shine,
You should have seen him gallop down the line
With hair astream! It warmed your blood to
      see
The way he clapped his hat beneath his knee
And yelled "Come on!" 'Go ask him if we
      came!'

And so they conjured with a magic name;
But, wakeful in the darkness after taps,
How many saddened, conscious of the lapse
Of man-denying time!

                  The last owl ceased.
A pewee sensed the changing of the east
And fluted shyly, doubtful of the news.
A wolf, returning from an all-night cruise
Among the rabbits, topped a staring rim
And vanished. Now the cooks were stirring
      dim,
Waist-deep in woodsmoke crawling through
      the damp.
The shadow lifted from the snoring camp.
The bugle sang. The horses cried ha! ha!
The mule herd raised a woeful fanfara
To swell the music, singing out of tune.
Up came the sun.

                  The Seventh marched at noon,
Six hundred strong. By fours and troop by
      troop,
With packs between, they passed the Colonel's
      group

By Terry's tent; the Rickarees and Crows
Astride their shaggy paints and calicoes;
The regimental banner and the grays;
And after them the sorrels and the bays,
The whites, the browns, the piebalds and the
    blacks.
One flesh they seemed with those upon their
    backs,
Whose weathered faces, like and fit for bronze,
Some gleam of unforgotten battle-dawns
Made bright and hard. The music of their
    going,
How good to hear!—though mournful beyond
    knowing;
The low-toned chanting of the Crows and Rees,
The guidons whipping in a stiff south breeze
Prophetical of thunder-brewing weather,
The chiming spurs and bits and crooning
    leather,
The shoe calks clinking on the scattered stone,
And, fusing all, the rolling undertone
Of hoofs by hundreds rhythmically blent—
The diapason of an instrument
Strung taut for battle music.

                      So they passed.
And Custer, waking from a dream at last
With still some glory of it in his eyes,
Shook hands around and said his last goodbyes
And swung a leg across his dancing bay
That champed the snaffle, keen to be away
Where all the others were. Then Gibbon
    spoke,
Jocosely, but with something in the joke

Of its own pleasantry incredulous:
"Now don't be greedy, Custer! Wait for us!"
And Custer laughed and gave the bay his head.
"I won't!" he cried. Perplexed at what he
    said,
They watched the glad bay smoking up the
    draw
And heard the lusty welcoming hurrah
That swept along the column. When it died,
The melancholy pack mules prophesied
And ghost-mules answered.

XII. HIGH NOON ON THE LITTLE HORN

                          Now it came to pass,
That late June morning on the Greasy Grass,
Two men went fishing, warriors of the Sioux;
And, lonesome in the silence of the two,
A youngster pictured battles on the sand.
Once more beneath the valor of his hand
The execrated troopers, blotted out,
Became a dust. Then, troubled with a doubt,
He ventured: "Uncle, will they find us here—
The soldiers?" 'Twas a buzzing in the ear
Of Red Hawk where he brooded on his cast.
"The wind is coming up," he said at last;
"The sky grows dusty." "Then the fish won't
      bite,"
Said Running Wolf. "There may be rain
      tonight"
Said Red Hawk, falling silent. Bravely then
The youngster wrought himself a world of men
Where nothing waited on a wind of whim,
But everything, obedient to him,
Fell justly. All the white men in the world
Were huddled there, and round about them
      swirled
More warriors than a grownup might surmise.
The pony-thunder and the battle-cries,
The whine of arrows eager for their marks
Drowned out the music of the meadowlarks,

The rising gale that teased the cottonwoods
To set them grumbling in their whitened hoods,
The chatter of a little waterfall.
These pebbles—see!—were Crazy Horse and
    Gall;
Here Crow King raged, and Black Moon
    battled there!
This yellow pebble—look!—was Yellow Hair;
This drab one with a little splotch of red,
The Gray Fox, Crook! Ho ho! And both
    were dead;
And white men fell about them every place—
The leafage of the autumn of a race—
Till all were down. And when their doom was
    sealed,
The little victor danced across the field
Amid the soundless singing of a throng.
The brief joy died, for there was something
    wrong
About this battle. Mournfully came back
That other picture of a dawn attack—
The giant horses rearing in the fogs
Of their own breath; the yelping of the dogs;
The screaming rabble swarming up the rise;
The tangled terror in his mother's eyes;
The flaming lodges and the bloody snow.
Provokingly oblivious of woe,
The two still eyed the waters and were dumb.

"But will they find us, Uncle? Will they
    come?"

Now Red Hawk grunted, heaving at his line,
And, wrought of flying spray and morning-
    shine,

A spiral rainbow flashed along the brook.
"*Hey hey!*" said Red Hawk, staring at his
    hook,
"He got my bait! Run yonder to the bluff
And catch some hoppers, Hohay. Get enough
And you shall see how fish are caught today!"

Half-heartedly the youngster stole away
Across a brawling riffle, climbed the steep
And gazed across the panoramic sweep
Of rolling prairie, tawny in the drouth,
To where the Big Horns loomed along the
    south,
No more than ghosts of mountains in the dust.
Up here the hot wind, booming gust on gust,
Made any nook a pleasant place to dream.
You could not see the fishers by the stream;
And you were grown so tall that, looking down
Across the trees, you saw most all the town
Strung far along the valley. First you saw
The Cheyennes yonder opposite the draw
That yawned upon the ford—a goodly sight!
So many and so mighty in a fight
And always faithful brothers to the Sioux!
Trees hid the Brulé village, but you knew
'Twas half a bow-shot long from end to end.
Then Ogalalas filled a river bend,
And next the Minneconjoux did the same.
A little farther south the Sans Arc came,
And they were neighbors to the Hunkpapas.—
The blackened smoke-vents, flapping in the
    flaws,
Were like a startled crow flock taking wing.—
Some Ogalalas played at toss-the-ring

And many idlers crowded round to see.—
The grazing ponies wandered lazily
Along the flat and up the rolling west.

Now, guiltily remembering his quest,
He trotted farther up the naked hill,
Dropped down a gully where the wind was
     still—
And came upon a hopping army there!
They swarmed, they raged—but Hohay didn't
     care;
For suddenly it seemed the recent climb
Had been a scramble up the height of time
And Hohay's name was terror in the ears
Of evil peoples. Seizing weeds for spears,
He charged the soldiers with a dreadful shout.
The snapping of their rifles all about
Might daunt a lesser hero. Never mind;
His medicine made all their bullets blind,
And 'twas a merry slaughter. Then at last
The shining glory of the vision passed,
And hoppers were but hoppers as before,
And he, a very little boy once more,
Stood dwarfed and lonely on a windy rise.
The sun was nearly up the dusty skies.
'Twas white with heat and had a funny stare—
All face! The wind had blown away its hair.
It looked afraid; as though the sun should fear!

Now, squinting downward through the flying
     blear,
He scanned the town. And suddenly the old
Remembered dawn of terror struck him cold.
Like startled ants that leave a stricken mound
In silence that is felt as panic sound

By one who sees, the squaws and children
    poured
Along the valley northward past the ford;
And men were chasing ponies every place,
While many others ran, as in a race,
To southward.

                Hohay, taking to his heels,
Made homeward like a cottontail that feels
A kiote pant and whimper at his tail.
He reached the bluff rim, scrambled to the
    vale
And crossed the stream. The fishermen were
    gone.
A hubbub in the village led him on
Pell-mell among the snatching underwood,
Till, checked as by a wall of sound, he stood
Apant and dripping in the howling town.

A bent old man there hobbled up and down
Upon a staff and sang a cackling song
Of how his heart was young again and strong;
But no one heeded. Women ran with guns
And bows and war clubs, screaming for their
    sons
And husbands. Men were mounting in a whirl
Of manes and tails to vanish in a swirl
Of scattered sand; and ever louder blew
The singing wind of warriors riding through
To battle. Hohay watched them, mouth agape,
Until he felt a hand upon his nape
That shoved him north, and someone shouted
    "Run!"
He scampered.

Meanwhile, nearer to the sun,
A rifle shot beyond the village end,
Came Reno's troopers pouring round a bend,
Their carbines ready at their saddle bows.
A bugle yammered and a big dust rose
And horses nickered as the fours swung wide
In battle order; and the captains cried,
And with a running thunder of hurrahs
The long line stormed upon the Hunkpapas
Strung thin across the open flat. They fled
Like feeble ghosts of men already dead
Beneath those hoofs; for now it seemed they saw
The yellow-headed Wolf of Washita
Already on their heels, with all his pack
Potential in the dust cloud at his back,
A howling fury!
                    Flame along a slough
Before a howling wind, the terror grew
As momently increased the flying mass,
For all the others running up were grass
Before that flame; till men became aware
Of how another voice was booming there,
Outsoaring Panic's, smashing through the
    brawl
Of hoofs and wind and rifles.

                         It was Gall.
A night wind blowing when the stars are dim,
His big black gelding panted under him;
And scarce he seemed a man of mortal race,
His naked body and his massive face
Serene as hewn from time-forgotten rock,
Despite the horse's rearing to the shock

[141]

Of surging men. Boy-hearted warriors took
New courage from the father in his look
And listened in a sudden lull of sound.
"The foe is there!" he shouted. "Turn
    around!
Die here today!" And everywhere he rode
A suck of men grew after him and flowed
To foeward.

                    Now it seemed the routed fear
Had joined the halted troops. They ceased to
    cheer.
Dismounting with their right upon the trees
Along the river, and the Rickarees
Upon their left, they flung a blazing dam
Across the valley. Like a river jam
The eager rabble deepened on the front,
For other hundreds, howling to the hunt,
Were dashing up with ponies. Then they say
A sound was heard as when a jam gives way
Before a heaped up freshet of the Spring,
And ponies in a torrent smote the wing
Where, mounted yet, the little Ree band stood.

Now those, remembering where life was good,
Regretting that they ever chose to roam
So far from kindly faces, started home
Without farewells; and round the crumpled
    flank
The Sioux came thronging, bending back the
    rank
Upon the pivot of the farther troop,
Till, crowded in a brushy river loup,
The soldiers fought bewildered and forlorn.
Behind them from across the Little Horn

The long range rifles on the bluff rim spat
A hornet swarm among them; and the flat
Before them swam with ponies on the run—
A vertigo of shadows; for the sun
Went moony in the dust and disappeared.
Inverted faces of a nightmare leered
Beneath the necks of ponies hurtling past;
And every surge of horsemen seemed the last,
So well their daring fed upon their rage.

It might have been a moment or an age
The troopers gripped that slipping edge of life,
When some along the left saw Bloody Knife,
By Reno, straighten from his fighting squat.
And heard him scream, and saw the wound he
      got
Spew brains between the fingers clutching there.
Then like a drowning man with hands in air
He sank. And some who fought nearby have
      said
The Major's face, all spattered with the red
Of that snuffed life, went chalky, and his shout
Scarce reached the nearer troopers round about:
"*Back to the bluffs!*" But when a few arose
To do his will, they say he raged at those:
"*Get down! Get down!*" Then once again he
      cried:
"*Get to the bluffs!*"—And was the first to ride.

Now some along the right, who had not heard,
But saw the mounting, passed a shouted word
That groped, a whisper, through the roaring
      smoke:
"We're going to charge!" And where it fell,
      it broke

The ragged line. Men scrambled to the rear
Where now the plunging horses shrieked with
    fear
And fought their holding "fours"—nor all in
    vain,
For whole quadrigæ, fastened bit to rein,
Ramped down that stormy twilight of the Sioux.
The nearest empty saddle seat would do
For any lucky finder. Rout or charge—
What matter? All along the river marge
The man storm raged, and all the darkened
    vale
Was tumult. To retreat was to assail,
Assault was flight. The craven and the bold
Seemed one that moment where the loud dust
    rolled,
Death-strewing, up along the Little Horn.

About the loup a mockery of morn
Broke in upon the gloaming of the noon,
And horseless troopers, starting from the swoon
Of battle, saw, and knew themselves alone
And heard the wounded wailing and the moan
Of dying men around them. Even these,
Forlorn among the bullet-bitten trees,
Were scarce less lucky than the fleeing ranks
With crowding furies snapping at their flanks,
Death in the rear and frantic hope ahead.
'Twas like a bison hunt, the Sioux have said,
When few bulls battle and the fat cows run
Less fleet than slaughter. Hidden from the sun,
How many a boy, struck motherless, belied
The whiskered cheek; what heroism died,
Fronting the wild white glory!

                                        Funk or fight,
Lost in the noon's anomaly of night,
The troopers struggled, groping for a ford.
But more and more the pressure of the horde
Bore leftward, till the steep-banked river spread
Before them, and the bluffs that loomed ahead
Were like the domes of heaven to the damned.
A shrinking moment, and the flood was jammed
With men and horses thrashing belly deep;
And down upon them, jostled to the leap,
The rear cascaded. Many-noted pain
Sang medley in the roaring rifle rain
That swept the jetting water, gust on gust.
And many a Sioux, gone wild with slaughter lust,
Plunged after. Madmen grappled in the flood,
And tumbling in the current, streaked with
      blood,
Drank deep together and were satisfied.

Now scrambling out upon the further side,
The hunted troopers blundered at a steep
More suited to the flight of mountain sheep
Than horses; for a narrow pony trail,
That clambered up a gully from the vale,
Immediately clogged with brutes and men.
Spent horses skittered back to strive again,
Red-flanked and broken-hearted. Many bore
Their riders where no horse had gone before,
Nor ever shall go. Bullets raked the slope,
And from the valley to the heights of hope
The air was dirty with the arrow-snow.
The heights of hope? Alas, that stair of woe,
Strewn with the bleeding offal of the rout,
Led only to an eminence of doubt,

A more appalling vision of their plight;
For in the rear and on the left and right
The nearer bluffs were filling with the Sioux,
And still along the flat beneath them blew
The dust of thousands yelping for the kill.

They say that good men broke upon the hill
And wept as children weep. And there were
      some
Who stared about them empty eyed and
      dumb,
As though it didn't matter. Others hurled
Profane irrelevancies at the world
Or raved about the jamming of their guns.
And yet there lacked not level-headed ones,
Unruffled shepherds of the flock, who strove
For order in the milling of the drove
With words to soothe or cheer, or sting with
      scorn.

Now up the valley of the Little Horn
Wild news came crying from the lower town
Of other soldiers yonder riding down
Upon the guardless village from the east;
And every tongue that sped the news increased
The meaning of it. Victory forsook
Big hearts that withered. Lo, the Gray Fox,
      Crook,
Returning for revenge—and not alone!
How many camps along the Yellowstone
Were emptied on the valley there below?
The whipped were but a sprinkle of the foe,
And now the torrent was about to burst!
With everything to know, they knew the worst,
And saw the clearer in that no one saw.

Then broke a flying area of awe
Across the rabble like a patch of sun
Upon the troubled corn when gray clouds run
And in the midst a glowing rift is blown.
Pressed back before the plunging white-faced
    roan
Of Crazy Horse, men brightened. How they
    knew
That lean, swift fighting-spirit of the Sioux,
The wizard eyes, the haggard face and thin,
Transfigured by a burning from within
Despite the sweat-streaked paint and battle
    grime!
Old men would ponder in the wane of time
That lifting vision and alluring cry:
"*There never was a better day to die!*
Come on, Dakotas!   Cowards to the rear!"

Some hundreds yonder held the net of fear
Round Reno's hill; but in the cloud that spread
Along the valley where the fleet roan led
Were thousands.

          Now the feeble and the young,
The mothers and the maidens, terror-flung
Beyond the lower village to the west,
Had seen the soldiers loom along a crest
Beyond the town, and, heading down a swale
By fours, with guidons streaming in the gale,
Approach the ford. 'Twas Custer with the grays,
A sorrel troop and thrice as many bays—
Two hundred and a handful at the most;
But 'twas the bannered onset of a host
To those who saw and fled. Nor could they know
The numbers and the valiance of the foe

Down river where the bulls of war were loud;
For even then that thunder and the cloud
Came northward. Were they beaten? Had
    they won?
What devastation, darkening the sun,
Was tearing down the valley? On it roared
And darkled; deepened at the lower ford
And veered cyclonic up the yawning draw
To eastward. Now the breathless people saw
The dusty ponies darting from the van
And swarming up the left. The guns began,
A running splutter. Yonder to the south
The big dust boiling at a coulee's mouth
Was pouring ponies up around the right.
Grown dimmer in the falling battle-night,
The stormy guidons of the troopers tossed,
Retreating upward, lessened and were lost
Amid a whirling cloud that topped the hill.
And steadily the valley spouted still
The double stream of warriors.

                            Then a shout
Enringed the battle, and the scene went out
In rumbling dust—as though a mine were lit
Beneath the summit and the belch of it
Gloomed bellowing. A windy gloaming spread
Across the ridges flicked with errant lead
And wayward arrows groping for a mark.
And horses, hurtled from the central dark,
With empty saddles charged upon the day.

Meanwhile on Reno's hill four miles away
Men heartened to a rousing cheer had seen
The bays and blacks and sorrels of Benteen,

Hoof-heavy with their unavailing quest
Among the valleys to the south and west,
Toil upward. Unmolested by the foe,
The pack mules, trumpeting "We told you so,"
Trudged in a little later. By the cheers
It might have been reunion after years;
And was in truth; for there were graying locks,
That night, to mock the pedantry of clocks,
Untroubled by the ages life can pack
Between the ticks.

           The fire had fallen slack
Upon the watching summits round about
And in a maze of wonderment and doubt
Men scanned the north that darkled as with war.
'What was it that the Major waited for?
He'd best be doing something pretty quick
Or there'd be Custer with a pointed stick
To look for him!' So growled a bolder few.
But many thought of little else to do
'Than just to dodge the leaden wasp that kills
Sent over by the snipers on the hills
In fitful swarms.

           Now like a bellowed word
The miles made inarticulate, they heard
A sound of volley-firing. *There! and there!*
Hoarse with a yet incredible despair
That incoherent cry of kin to kin
Grew big above the distant battle din—
The sequent breakers of a moaning sea.
And twice the murmuring veil of mystery
Was rent and mended. Then the tearing drawl
Was heard no more where Fury, striding tall,
Made one in dust the heavens and the earth.

'He's pitching into them for all he's worth,'
Some ventured;—'was there nothing else to do
But hug that hill?'

     Then suddenly there grew
A voice of wrath, and many lying near,
Who heard it, looked—and it was Captain
  Wier
By Reno yonder; and the place went still:
"Then, Major, if you won't, by God I will,
And there'll be more to say if we get back!"
They saw him fling a leg across his black
And take the northward steep with face set
  grim;
And all the black horse troop rode after him
Across the gulch to vanish on a rise.

Two miles away from where the smudgy skies
Of afternoon anticipated night,
They halted on a space-commanding height
And, squinting through the dusty air ahead,
Were puzzled. For the silence of the dead
Had fallen yonder—only now and then
A few shots crackled. Groups of mounted men—
Not troopers—by the rifting dust revealed,
Were scattered motionless about the field,
As wearily contented with a work
Well done at last.

     Then suddenly the murk
Began to boil and murmur, like a storm
Before the wind comes. Ponies in a swarm
Were spreading out across the ridgy land
Against the blacks.

By now the whole command
Was coming up, and not a whit too soon;
For once again the sun became a moon
Amid the dust of thousands bearing down.

Now farther back upon a bleak bluff crown
The troop of Godfrey waited for the fight,
Not doubting that their comrades held the right,
When orders, riding with an urgent heel,
Arrived with more of prudence to reveal
Than pluck: *Withdraw at once!* A startled stare
Made plain how all the flanking hills were bare
And not a sign of Reno in the rear!
Just then the fleeing troops of French and Wier
Came roaring down across a ridge in front
And, close upon their heels, the howling hunt
Made dimmer yet the summit of the slope.
And Godfrey, seeing very little hope
If all should flee those thousands, overjoyed
With some great *coup*, dismounted and de-
    ployed
To fight on foot, and sent the horses back.
And so he dared the brunt of the attack,
Retreating slowly like a wounded bear
With yelping dogs before him everywhere
Regardful of the eager might at bay.
And so the whole command got back that day
Of big despairs; and men remember still.

Then all the ridges circling Reno's hill
Were crowded. In among the flattened men,
Now desperately fighting one to ten,
Hell hornets snarled and feathered furies
    crooned
A death song; and the sun was like a wound

Wherewith the day bled dizzy. Yet from all
The muddled nightmare of it, men recall
Deeds brighter for the years: how Captain
    French,
Like any stodgy tailor on his bench,
Sat cross-legged at the giddy edge of life
Serenely picking with a pocket knife
The shell-jammed guns and loading them anew;
How, seemingly enamoured of the view,
Deliberate, Johnsonian of mien,
His briar drawing freely, strolled Benteen
Along his fighting line; how Wallace, Wier
And Godfrey yonder, fearing only fear,
Walked round among the troopers, cheering
    them.
And some remember Happy Jack of M,
The way his gusty laughter served to melt
The frost of terror, though the joy he felt
Seemed less to mark a hero than a fool.
And once, they say, an ammunition mule
Broke loose and bolted, braying, as he went,
Defiance and a traitorous intent
To quit the Whites forever. Then they tell
How Sergeant Hanley with an Irish yell
Took horse and followed, jealous for the pack;
And all the line roared after him, "Come back!
Come back, you fool!" But Hanley went
    ahead.
At times you hardly saw him for the lead
That whipped the dust up. Blindly resolute,
The traitor with the Irish in pursuit
Struck up along a hostile ridge that burned
And smoked and bellowed. Presently he turned
And panted home, an image of remorse;

And Hanley, leaping from his winded horse,
Lay down and went to work among the rest.

The wounded day bled ashen in the west;
The firing dwindled in the dusk and ceased;
The frightened stars came peeking from the east
To see what anguish moaned. The wind went
    down—
A lull of death. But yonder in the town
All night the war drums flouted that despair
Upon the hill, and dancers in the glare
Of fires that towered filled the painted dark
With demon exultation, till the lark
Of doom should warble. Heavy-lidded eyes
Saw often in the sage along a rise
The loom of troops. If any shouted "Look!"
And pointed, all the others cheered for Crook
Or Terry coming; and the bugles cried
To mocking echoes. When the sick hope died,
They fell to sullen labor, scraping up
The arid earth with plate and drinking cup
Against the dreaded breaking of the day.
And here and there among the toilers lay
The winners of an endless right to shirk;
While many panted at a harder work,
The wage whereof is nothing left to buy.

It seemed that all were men about to die,
Forlornly busy there among the dead—
Each man his sexton. Petulant with dread,
They talked of Custer, grumbling at a name
Already shaping on the lips of Fame
To be a deathless bugle-singing soon.
For no one guessed what now the tardy moon

Was poring over with a face of fright
Out yonder: naked bodies gleaming white
The whole way to the summit of the steep
Where Silence, brooding on a tumbled heap
Of men and horses, listened for a sound. . . .
A wounded troop horse sniffed the bloody
    ground
And ghosts of horses nickered when he neighed.

Now scarcely had the prairie owls, afraid
Of morning, ceased, or waiting hushes heard
A timid, unauthoritative bird
Complain how late the meadowlarks awoke,
When suddenly the dreaded fury broke
About the sleepless troopers, digging still.
It raked the shallow trenches on the hill;
It beat upon the little hollow where
The mules and horses, tethered in a square
About the wounded, roared and plunged amain,
Tight-tailed against no pasture-loving rain;
And many fell and floundered. What of night
From such a morning? For the hostile light
Increased the fury, and the battle grew.

That day it seemed the very sun was Sioux.
The heat, the frenzy and the powder gas
Wreaked torture. Men were chewing roots of
    grass
For comfort ere the day had well begun.
Bare to the grim mid-malice of the sun,
The wounded raved for water. Far below,
Cool with the melting of the mountain snow,
The river gleamed; and, queasy with the smell
Of bodies bloating in a stew of hell,

Men croaked about it. Better to be killed
Half way to yonder joy than perish grilled
Between that grid of earth and burning air!

So nineteen troopers volunteered to dare
A grisly race. The twentieth who ran,
Invisible and fleeter than a man,
With hoofs of peril flicked the dusty sod
Where pluckily the sprinting water squad
Made streamward. Giddy with a wound he got,
A trooper tumbled, and his cooking pot
Pursued the others with a bounding roll.
A second runner crumpled near the goal.
And when the sprawling winners drank, they
    say
The bullets whipped the water into spray
About their heads; for yonder in the brush
The Sioux kept watch, but dared not make a
    rush
Because of marksmen stationed on the bluff.
And when the greedy drinkers had enough,
With brimming kettles and the filled canteens
They toiled along the tortuous ravines
And panted up a height that wasn't Fame's.
Men still recall the water; but the names
Enrich that silence where the millions go.

The shadows had begun to overflow
Their stagnant puddles on the nightward side,
When presently the roar of battle died
On all the circling summits there. Perplexed
With what the wily foe might purpose next,
The troopers lay and waited. Still the swoon
Of silence held the stifling afternoon,

Save for a low monotony of pain,
The keening of the gnats about the slain
That festered. Nothing happened. Shadows
    crept
A little farther nightward. Many slept,
Dead to the sergeant's monitory shake;
And some, for very weariness awake,
Got up and dared to stretch a leg at last,
When from the summits broke a rifle blast
That banished sleep and drove the strollers in.

Abruptly as it started, ceased the din
And all the hills seemed empty as before.

And, breath by breath, the weary waiting wore
The hours out. Every minute, loath to pass,
Forewarned the next of some assault in mass
Preparing in the hush. A careless head
Above a horse's carcass drew the lead
Of lurking marksmen. What would be the
    end?
The prayed-for dark itself might prove no
    friend
For all its pity.

                    Now the early slant
Of evening made the thirsty horses pant
And raise a running whimper of despair,
When, seemingly ignited by the glare,
The very prairie smouldered. Spire by spire,
Until the whole fat valley was afire,
Smoke towered in the windless air and grew
Where late the league long village of the Sioux
Lay hidden from the watchers on the hill;
And like the shadow of a monster ill

Untimely gloaming fell across the height.
Yet nothing but the failing of the light
Upon the distant summits came to pass.
The muffled murmur of the burning grass
Was all the reeking valley had of sound;
And when the troopers dared to walk around,
No spluttering of rifles drove them back.

The shadows in the draws were getting black
When someone lifted up a joyous cry
That set the whole band staring where the sky,
To southward of the smoke, remembered day.
And there they saw, already miles away—
A pictographic scrawl upon the glow—
The tangled slant and clutter of travaux
By crowding hundreds; ponies that pursued,
A crawling, milling, tossing multitude,
A somber river brawling out of banks;
And glooms of horsemen flowing on the
     flanks—
The whole Sioux village fleeing with the light
To where the Big Horn Mountains glimmered
     white
And low along the south!

                    The horses neighed
To swell the happy noise their masters made.
The pack mules sang the only song they knew.
And summits, late familiar with the Sioux,
Proclaimed a new allegiance, cheer on cheer.
For who could doubt that news of Terry near
Had driven off the foe?

XIII. THE TWILIGHT

                    A moon wore by,
And in the rainless waning of July
Ten thousand hearts were troubled where the
     creeks,
Young from the ancient winter of the peaks,
Romped in the mountain meadows green as
     May.
The very children lost the heart to play,
Awed by the shadow of an unseen thing,
As covies, when the shadow of a wing
Forebodes a pounce of terror from the skies.
They saw it in the bravest father's eyes—
That shadow—in the gentlest mother's face;
Unwitting how there fell upon a race
The twilight of irreparable wrong.
The drums had fallen silent with the song,
And valiant tales, late eager to be told,
Were one with all things glorious and old
And dear and gone forever from the Sioux.

For now the hunted prairie people knew
How powerful the Gray Fox camp had
     grown
On Goose Creek; how along the Yellowstone
The mounted soldiers and the walking ones—
A multitude—had got them wagon guns,

Of which the voice was thunder and the stroke,
Far off, a second thunder and a smoke
That bit and tore. A little while, and then
Those open jaws, toothed terribly with men,
Would move together, closing to the bite.
What hope was left in anything but flight?
And whither? O the world was narrow now!
South, east, the rat-like nibbling of the plow
Had left them but a little way to go.
The mountains of the never melting snow
Walled up the west. Beyond the northern haze.
There lay a land of unfamiliar ways,
Dark tongues and alien eyes.

                              As waters keep
Their wonted channels, yearning for the deep,
The homeless rabble took the ancient road.
From bluff to bluff the Rosebud valley flowed
Their miles of ponies; and the pine-clad heights
Were sky-devouring torches in the nights
Behind them, and a rolling gloom by day;
And prairies, kindled all along the way,
Bloomed balefully and blackened. Noon was
      dark,
Night starless, and the fleeing meadowlark
Forgot the morning. Where the Bluestone runs
Their dust bore east; and seldom did the suns
Behold them going for the seed they strewed
To crop the rearward prairie solitude
With black starvation even for the crow.
Creeks, stricken as with fever, ceased to flow
And languished in a steaming ashen mire.
But more than grass was given to the fire—
O memories no spring could render young!

And so it was that, marching down the Tongue,
The Gray Fox, seeking for the hostile bands,
Saw nothing but the desolated lands
Black to the sky; and when a dreary week
Had brought him to the mouth of Bluestone
      Creek,
Lo, Terry with another empty tale!

Broad as a road to ruin ran the trail
Of driven pony herds, a livid scar
Upon a vast cadaver, winding far
To eastward as the tallest hill might look.
And thither pressed the horse and foot of Crook,
Their pack mules, lighter for a greater speed,
With scant provisions for a fortnight's need
Upon their saddles.

                    Burning August waned
About the toiling regiments. It rained—
A sodden, chill monotony of rains—
As though the elements had cursed the plains,
And now that flame had stricken, water struck.
The scarecrow horses struggled with the suck
Of gumbo flats and heartbreak hills of clay;
And many a bone-bag fell beside the way
Too weak to rise, for still the draws were few
That were not blackened. Crows and buz-
      zards knew
How little eager claws and whetted beaks
Availed them where so many hollow cheeks
Had bulged about a brief and cookless feast.

Still wearily the main trail lengthened east
By hungry days and fireless bivouacs;
And more and more diverging pony tracks,

To north and south, and tangent lodge pole trails
Revealed the hunted scattering as quails
Before a dreaded hunter. Eastward still
They staggered, nourished by a doggéd will,
Past where a little river apes in mud
And name the genius of a titan flood
That drinks it. Crumbling pinnacles of awe
Looked down upon them; domes of wonder saw
The draggled column slowly making head
Against the muck; the drooping horses, led,
Well loaded with their saddles; empty packs,
Become a cruel burden on the backs
Of plodding mules with noses to the ground.
Along the deeps of Davis Creek they wound,
To where the Camel's Hump and Rosebud
      Butte
Behold the Heart's head.

                    Here the long pursuit,
It seemed, had come to nothing after all.
The multitude of Crazy Horse and Gall
Had vanished in that God-forsaken place
And matched their fagged pursuers for a race
With something grimmer than a human foe.
Four marches east across the dim plateau
Fort Lincoln lured them. Twice as many days
Beyond the dripping low September haze,
Due south across the yet uncharted lands,
Lay Deadwood, unprotected from the bands
Of prowling hostiles. 'Twas enough for Crook.
Half-heartedly the ragged column took
The way of duty.

                    And the foe appeared!
Where, like a god-built stadium, the tiered

Age-carven Slim Buttes watch the Rabbit's Lip
Go groping for the ocean, in the drip
And ooze of sodden skies the battle raged;
And presences, millennially aged
In primal silence, shouted at the sight.
Until the rifles gashed the front of night
With sanguinary wounds, they fought it out;
And darkness was the end of it, and doubt
And drizzle. Unrejoicing victors knew
What enemy, more mighty than the Sioux,
Would follow with no lagging human feet;
And early morning saw them in retreat
Before that foe. Above their buried slain
A thousand horses trampled in the rain
That none might know the consecrated ground
To violate it.

        Up and up they wound
Among the foggy summits, till the van
Was checked with awe. Inimical to Man,
Below them spread a featureless immense,
More credibly a dream of impotence
Than any earthly country to be crossed—
A gloomy flat, illimitably lost
In gauzes of the downpour.

        Thither strove
The gaunt battalions. And the chill rain drove
Unceasingly. Through league on league of mire
Men straggled into camps without a fire
To wolf their slaughtered horses in the red;
And all the wallow of the way they fled
Was strewn with crowbaits dying in the bogs.
About them in the forest of the fogs

[162]

Lurked Crazy Horse, a cougar mad for blood;
And scarce the rearguard-battles in the mud
Aroused the sullen plodders to the fore.
TheDeer'sEars loomed and vanished in the pour;
The Haystack Buttes stole off along the right;
And men grew old between a night and night
Before their feeble toil availed to raise
The Black Hills, set against the evil days
About a paradise of food and rest.

Now Crazy Horse's people, turning west,
Retraced the trail of ruin, sick for home.
Where myriads of the bison used to roam
And fatten in the golden autumn drowse,
A few rejected bulls and barren cows
Grew yet a little leaner.   Every place
The good old earth, with ashes on her face,
Was like a childless mother in despair;
Though still she kept with jealous, loving care
Some little hoard of all her youth had known
Against the dear returning of her own;
But where the starving herd of ponies passed,
The little shielded hollows, lately grassed,
Were stricken barren even as with fire.
And so they reached the place of their desire,
The deep-carved valley where the Powder flows.
Here surely there was peace.

                 But when the snows
Came booming where the huddled village stood
And ponies, lean with gnawing cottonwood,
Were slain to fill the kettles, Dull Knife came,
The great Cheyenne. The same—O not the same
As he who fought beside the Greasy Grass
And slew his fill of enemies! Alas,

The beggar in his eyes! And very old
He seemed, for hunger and the pinch of cold
Were on him; and the rabble at his back—
Despairing hundreds—lacked not any lack
That flesh may know and live. The feeble wail
Of babies put an edge upon the tale
That Dull Knife told.

              "There was a fight" he said.
"I set my winter village at the head
Of Willow Creek. The mountains there are tall.
A canyon stood about me for a wall;
And it was good to hear my people sing,
For there was none that wanted anything
That makes men happy. We were all asleep.
The cold was sharp; the snow was very deep.
What enemy could find us? We awoke.
A thunder and a shouting and a smoke
Were there among us, and a swarm of foes—
Pawnees, Shoshones and Arapahoes,
And soldiers, many soldiers. It was night
About us, and we fought them in the light
Of burning lodges till the town was lost
And all our plenty. Bitter was the frost
And most of us were naked from the bed.
Now many of our little ones are dead
Of cold and hunger. Shall the others die?"

There was a light in Crazy Horse's eye
Like moony ice. The other spoke again.
"As brothers have Dakota and Cheyenne
Made war together. Help us. You have seen
We can not live until the grass is green,
My brother!"

Then the other face grew stone;
The hard lips moved: "A man must feed his
    own,"
Said Crazy Horse, and turned upon his heel.
But now the flint of him had found the steel
In Dull Knife, and the flare was bad to see.
"Tashunka Witko, dare to look at me
That you may not forget me. We shall meet.
The soldiers yonder have enough to eat,
And I will come, no beggar, with the grass!"

And silently the people saw him pass
Along the valley where the snow lay blue,
The plodding, silent, ragamuffin crew
Behind him. So the evil days began.

Now Crazy Horse, they say, was like a man
Who, having seen a ghost, must look and look
And brood upon the empty way it took
To nowhere; and he scarcely ate at all;
And there was that about him like a wall
To shut men out. He seemed no longer young.

Bleak January found them on the Tongue
In search of better forage for the herd—
A failing quest. And hither came the word
Of many walking soldiers coming down
With wagon guns upon the starving town
That might not flee; for whither could they go
With ponies pawing feebly in the snow
To grow the leaner? Mighty in despair,
They waited on a lofty summit there
Above the valley.

                    Raw gray dawn revealed
A scaly serpent crawling up a field

Of white beneath them. Leisurely it neared,
Resolving into men of frosty beard
With sloping rifles swinging to the beat
And melancholy fifing of their feet
Upon the frost; and shrill the wagon tires
Sang rearward. Now the soldiers lighted fires
And had their breakfast hot, as who should say:
"What hurry? It is early in the day
And there is time for what we came to do."
With wistful eyes the rabble of the Sioux
Beheld the eating; knew that they defied
In vain their own misgivings when they cried:
"Eat plenty! You will never eat again!"
It was not so; for those were devil men
Who needed nothing and were hard to kill.

The wagon-guns barked sharply at the hill
To bite the summit, always shooting twice;
And scrambling upward through the snow and
      ice
Came doggedly, without a sign of fear,
The infantry of Miles. They didn't cheer,
They didn't hurry, and they didn't stop,
For all the rifles roaring at the top,
Until the gun-butt met the battle-ax.
Still fighting with their children at their backs
The Sioux gave slowly. Wind came on to blow,
A hurrying northwester, blind with snow,
And in the wild white dusk of it they fled.

But when they reached the Little Powder's
      head,
So much of all their little had been lost,
So well had wrought their hunger and the frost,

One might have thought 'twas Dull Knife
    coming there.
The country had a cold, disowning stare;
The burned-off valleys could not feed their own.

The moon was like a frozen bubble, blown
Along the rim of February nights,
When Spotted Tail, the lover of the Whites,
Came there with mighty words. His cheeks
    were full,
IIis belly round. He spoke of Sitting Bull
And Gall defeated, driven far away
Across the line; of Red Cloud getting gray
Before his time—a cougar in a cage,
Self-eaten by a silent, toothless rage
That only made the watching sentry smile.
And still the story saddened. All the while
The scattered Sioux were coming in to save
Their children with the food the soldiers gave
And laying down their guns and making peace.
He told how Dull Knife's fury did not cease
But grew upon the soldier food he ate;
And how his people fattened, nursing hate
For Crazy Horse. And many more than these
But waited for the grass—the Loup Pawnees,
The Utes, the Winnebagoes and the Crows,
Shoshones, Bannocks and Arapahoes,
With very many more Dakotas too!

"Now what could Crazy Horse's people do
Against them all?" said Spotted Tail, the Wise.
And with the ancient puzzle in his eyes
That only death may riddle; gazing long
Now first upon the fat one in the wrong

And now upon the starving in the right,
The other found an answer: "I could fight!
And I could fight till all of us were dead.
But now I have no powder left," he said;
"I can not fight. Tell Gray Fox what you
    saw;
That I am only waiting for a thaw
To bring my people in."

XIV. THE DEATH OF CRAZY HORSE

                   And now 'twas done.
Spring found the waiting fort at Robinson
A half-moon ere the Little Powder knew;
And, doubting still what Crazy Horse might
    do
When tempted by the herald geese a-wing
To join the green rebellion of the spring,
The whole frontier was troubled. April came,
And once again his undefeated name
Rode every wind. Ingeniously the West
Wrought verities from what the East had
    guessed
Of what the North knew. Eagerly deceived,
The waiting South progressively believed
The wilder story. April wore away;
Fleet couriers, arriving day by day
With but the farthing mintage of the fact,
Bought credit slowly in that no one lacked
The easy gold of marvelous surmise.
For, gazing northward where the secret skies
Were moody with a coming long deferred,
Whoever spoke of Crazy Horse, still heard
Ten thousand hoofs.

                But yonder, with the crow
And kiote to applaud his pomp of woe,
The last great Sioux rode down to his defeat.
And now his people huddled in the sleet

Where Dog Creek and the Little Powder met.
With faces ever sharper for the whet
Of hunger, silent in the driving rains,
They straggled out across the blackened plains
Where Inyan Kara, mystically old,
Drew back a cloudy curtain to behold,
Serene with Time's indifference to men.
And now they tarried on the North Cheyenne
To graze their feeble ponies, for the news
Of April there had wakened in the sloughs
A glimmering of pity long denied.
Nor would their trail across the bare divide
Grow dimmer with the summer, for the bleach
Of dwindled herds—so hard it was to reach
The South Cheyenne. O sad it was to hear
How all the pent-up music of the year
Surged northward there the way it used to
    do!
In vain the catbird scolded at the Sioux;
The timid pewee queried them in vain;
Nor might they harken to the whooping crane
Nor heed the high geese calling them to
    come.
Unwelcome waifs of winter, drab and dumb,
Where ecstacy of sap and thrill of wing
Made shift to flaunt some color or to sing
The birth of joy, they toiled a weary way.
And giddy April sobered into May
Before they topped the summit looking down
Upon the valley of the soldier's town
At Robinson.

        Then eerily began
Among the lean-jowled warriors in the van

The chant of peace, a supplicating wail
That spread along the clutter of the trail
Until the last bent straggler sang alone;
And camp dogs, hunger-bitten to the bone,
Accused the heavens with a doleful sound;
But, silent still, with noses to the ground,
The laden ponies toiled to cheat the crows,
And famine, like a wag, had made of those
A grisly jest.
                    So Crazy Horse came in
With twice a thousand beggars.
                                        And the din
Died out, though here and there a dog still
        howled,
For now the mighty one, whom Fate had fouled,
Dismounted, faced the silent double row
Of soldiers haughty with the glint and glow
Of steel and brass. A little while he stood
As though bewildered in a haunted wood
Of men and rifles all astare with eyes.
They saw a giant shrunken to the size
Of any sergeant. Now he met the glare
Of Dull Knife and his warriors waiting there
With fingers itching at the trigger-guard.
How many comrade faces, strangely hard,
Were turned upon him! Ruefully he smiled,
The doubtful supplication of a child
Caught guilty; loosed the bonnet from his head
And cast it down. "I come for peace," he said;
"Now let my people eat." And that was all.

The summer ripened. Presages of fall
Now wanted nothing but the goose's flight.
The goldenrods had made their torches bright

Against the ghostly imminence of frost.
And one, long brooding on a birthright lost,
Remembered and remembered. O the time
When all the prairie world was white with rime
Of mornings, and the lodge smoke towered
    straight
To meet the sunlight, coming over late
For happy hunting! O the days, the days
When winds kept silence in the far blue haze
To hear the deep-grassed valleys running full
With fatling cows, and thunders of the bull
Across the hills! Nights given to the feast
When big round moons came smiling up the east
To listen to the drums, the dancing feet,
The voices of the women, high and sweet
Above the men's!

           And Crazy Horse was sad.
There wasn't any food the white man had
Could find his gnawing hunger and assuage.
Some saw a blood-mad panther in a cage,
And some the sulking of a foolish pride,
For there were those who watched him
    narrow-eyed
The whole day long and listened for a word,
To shuttle in the warp of what they heard
A woof of darker meaning.

             Then one day
A flying tale of battles far away
And deeds to make men wonder stirred the land:
How Nez Perce Joseph led his little band,
With Howard's eager squadrons in pursuit,
Across the mountains of the Bitter Root

To Big Hole Basin and the day-long fight;
And how his women, fleeing in the night,
Brought off the ponies and the children too.
O many a heart beat fast among the Sioux
To hear the way he fled and fought and fled
Past Bannack, down across the Beaverhead
To Henry's Lake, relentlessly pursued;
Now swallowed by the dreadful solitude
Where still the Mighty Spirit shapes the
    dream
With primal fires and prodigies of steam,
As when the fallow night was newly sown;
Now reappearing down the Yellowstone,
Undaunted yet and ever making less
That thousand miles of alien wilderness
Between a people's freedom and their need!

O there was virtue in the tale to feed
The withered heart and make it big again!
Not yet, not yet the ancient breed of men
Had vanished from the aging earth! They say
There came a change on Crazy Horse the day
The Ogalala village buzzed the news.
So much to win and only life to lose;
The bison making southward with the fall,
And Joseph fighting up the way to Gall
And Sitting Bull!

                    Who knows the dream he had?
Much talk there was of how his heart was bad
And any day some meditated deed
Might start an irresistible stampede
Among the Sioux—a human prairie-fire!
So back and forth along the talking wire

Fear chattered.   Yonder, far away as morn,
The mighty heard—and heard the Little Horn
Still roaring with the wind of Custer's doom.
And there were troopers moving in the gloom
Of midnight to the chaining of the beast;
But when the white light broke along the east,
There wasn't any Ogalala town
And Crazy Horse had vanished!

                                        Up and down
The dusty autumn panic horsemen spurred
Till all the border shuddered at the word
Of how that terror threatened every trail.

They found him in the camp of Spotted Tail,
A lonely figure with a face of care.
"I am afraid of what might happen there"
He said.   "So many listen what I say
And look and look.   I will not run away.
I want my people here.   You have my guns."

But half a world away the mighty ones
Had spoken words like bullets in the dark
That wreak the rage of blindness on a mark
They can not know.

                              Then spoke the one who led
The soldiers: "Not a hair upon your head
Shall suffer any harm if you will go
To Robinson for just a day or so
And have a parley with the soldier chief."
He spoke believing and he won belief,
So Crazy Horse went riding down the west;
And neither he nor any trooper guessed
What doom now made a rutted wagon road
The highway to a happier abode

Where all the dead are splendidly alive
And summer lingers and the bison thrive
Forever.

   If the better hope be true,
There was a gate of glory yawning through
The sunset when the little cavalcade
Approached the fort.

     The populous parade,
The straining hush that somehow wasn't peace,
The bristling troops, the Indian police
Drawn up as for a battle! What was wrong?
What made them hustle Crazy Horse along
Among the gleaming bayonets and eyes?
There swept a look of quizzical surprise
Across his face. He struggled with the guard.
Their grips were steel; their eyes were cold and
  hard—
Like bayonets.

    There was a door flung wide.
The soldier chief would talk with him inside
And all be well at last!

     The stifling, dim
Interior poured terror over him.
He blinked about—and saw the iron bars.

O nevermore to neighbor with the stars
Or know the simple goodness of the sun!
Did some swift vision of a doom begun
Reveal the monstrous purpose of a lie—
The desert island and the alien sky,
The long and lonely ebbing of a life?

The glimmer of a whipped-out butcher knife
Dismayed the shrinking squad, and once again
Men saw a face that many better men
Had died to see! Brown arms that once were
    kind,
A comrade's arms, whipped round him from
    behind,
Went crimson with a gash and dropped aside.
"Don't touch me! I am Crazy Horse!" he
    cried,
And, leaping doorward, charged upon the world
To meet the end. A frightened soldier hurled
His weight behind a jabbing belly-thrust,
And Crazy Horse plunged headlong in the dust,
A writhing heap. The momentary din
Of struggle ceased. The people, closing in,
Went ominously silent for a space,
And one could hear men breathing round the
    place
Where lay the mighty. Now he strove to rise,
The wide blind stare of anguish in his eyes,
And someone shouted *"Kill that devil quick!"*

A throaty murmur and a running click
Of gun-locks woke among the crowding Sioux,
And many a soldier whitened. Well they knew
What pent-up hate the moment might release
To drop upon the bungled farce of peace
A bloody curtain.

                    One began to talk;
His tongue was drunken and his face was chalk;
But when a halfbreed shouted what he spoke
The crowd believed, so few had seen the stroke,

Nor was there any bleeding of the wound.
It seemed the chief had fallen sick and swooned;
Perhaps a little rest would make him strong!
And silently they watched him borne along,
A sagging bundle, dear and mighty yet,
Though from the sharp face, beaded with the
    sweat
Of agony, already peered the ghost.

They laid him in an office of the post,
And soldiers, forming in a hollow square,
Held back the people. Silence deepened there.
A little while it seemed the man was dead,
He lay so still. The west no longer bled;
Among the crowd the dusk began to creep.
Then suddenly, as startled out of sleep
By some old dream-remembered night alarm,
He strove to shout, half rose upon an arm
And glared about him in the lamp-lit place.

The flare across the ashes of his face
Went out. He spoke; and, leaning where he
    lay,
Men strained to gather what he strove to say,
So hard the panting labor of his words.
"I had my village and my pony herds
On Powder where the land was all my own.
I only wanted to be let alone.
I did not want to fight. The Gray Fox sent
His soldiers. We were poorer when they went;
Our babies died, for many lodges burned
And it was cold. We hoped again and turned
Our faces westward. It was just the same
Out yonder on the Rosebud. Gray Fox came.

The dust his soldiers made was high and long.
I fought him and I whipped him. Was it
      wrong
To drive him back? That country was my
      own.
I only wanted to be let alone.
I did not want to see my people die.
They say I murdered Long Hair and they lie.
His soldiers came to kill us and they died."

He choked and shivered, staring hungry-eyed
As though to make the most of little light.
Then like a child that feels the clutching
      night
And cries the wilder, deeming it in vain,
He raised a voice made lyrical with pain
And terror of a thing about to be.
*"I want to see you, Father! Come to me!
I want to see you, Mother!"* O'er and o'er
His cry assailed the darkness at the door;
And from the gloom beyond the hollow square
Of soldiers, quavered voices of despair:
"We can not come! They will not let us come!"

But when at length the lyric voice was dumb
And Crazy Horse was nothing but a name,
There was a little withered woman came
Behind a bent old man. Their eyes were dim.
They sat beside the boy and fondled him,
Remembering the little names he knew
Before the great dream took him and he grew
To be so mighty. And the woman pressed
A hand that men had feared against her breast
And swayed and sang a little sleepy song.

Out yonder in the village all night long
There was a sound of mourning in the dark.
And when the morning heard the meadowlark,
The last great Sioux rode silently away.
Before the pony-drag on which he lay
An old man tottered.   Bowed above the bier,
A little wrinkled woman kept the rear
With not a sound and nothing in her eyes.

Who knows the crumbling summit where he lies
Alone among the badlands? Kiotes prowl
About it, and the voices of the owl
Assume the day-long sorrow of the crows,
These many grasses and these many snows.

THE SONG OF THE MESSIAH

I

THE VOICE IN THE WILDERNESS

The Earth was dying slowly, being old.
A grandam, crouched against an inner cold
Above the scraped-up ashes of the dear,
She babbled still the story of the year
By hopeless moons; but all her bloom was snow.
Mere stresses in a monody of woe,
Her winters stung the moment, and her springs
Were only garrulous rememberings
Of joy that made them sadder than the fall.
And mournful was the summer, most of all,
With fruitfulness remembered—bounteous sap
For happy giving, toddlers in her lap
And nuzzlers at her breast, and more to be,
And lovers eager still, so dear was she,
So needed and so beautiful to woo!

Ten years had grown the sorrow of the Sioux,
Blood-sown of one ingloriously slain,[1]
Whose dusty heart no sorcery of rain

[1] Crazy Horse.

Would sprout with pity, flowering for his own;
Nor could the blizzard's unresolving moan
Remind him of his people unconsoled.
Old as the earth, the hearts of men were old
That year of 'eighty-seven in the spring.

O once it was a very holy thing,
Some late March night, to waken to the moan
Of little waters, when the South, outblown,
Had left the soft dark clear of other sound;
When you could feel things waking underground
And all the world turned spirit, and you heard
Still thunders of the everlasting Word
Straining the hush.—Alas, to lie awake
Remembering, when time is like the ache
Of silence wedded, barren, to a wraith!

True to an empty ritual of faith,
The geese came chanting as they used to do
When there was wonder yet; when, blue on blue,
The world was wider than a day in June,
And twice the northbound bison lost the moon
Trailing the summer up the Sioux domain.
What myriads now would hear the whooping
        crane
And join the green migration?

                              Vision, sound,
Song from the green and color from the ground,
Scent in the wind and shimmer on the wing,

A cruel beauty, haunting everything,
Disguised the empty promise. In the sloughs
The plum brush, crediting the robin's news,
Made honey of it, and the bumblebee
Hummed with the old divine credulity
The music of the universal hoax.
Among the public cottonwoods and oaks
The shrill jays coupled and the catbird screamed,
Delirious with the dream the old Earth dreamed
Of ancient nuptials, ecstasies that were.
For once again the warm Rain over her
Folded the lover's blanket; nights were whist
To hear her low moan running in the mist,
Her secret whispers in the holy dark.
And every morning the deluded lark
Sang hallelujah to a widowed world.

May sickened into June. The short-grass curled.
Of evenings thunder mumbled 'round the sky;
But clouds were phantoms and the dawns were
    dry,
And it were better nothing had been born.
Sick-hearted in the squalor of the corn,
Old hunters brooded, dreaming back again
The days when earth still bore the meat of
    men—
Bull-thunders in a sky-wide storm of cows!—
Till bow-grips tightened on the hated plows
And spear-hands knuckled for an empty thrust.

The corn-stalks drooping in the bitter dust,
Despairing mothers widowed in the silk,
With swaddled babies dead for want of milk,
Moaned to the wind the universal dearth.

There was no longer magic in the earth;
No mystery was vital in the air;
No spirit in the silence anywhere
Made doubly sure a wonder that was sure.
To live was now no more than to endure
The purposeless indignity of breath,
Sick for the brave companion that was Death,
Now grown a coward preying on the weak.
However might the hungry-hearted seek
Upon a starry hill, however high,
A knowing Presence, everywhere the sky
Was like a tepee where the man lies stark
And women wail and babble in the dark
Of what the dawn can never bring to light.

The big Cheyenne lay dying, and the White;
And all the little creeks forgot their goals.
Crows feasted by the dusty water-holes.
Gaunt grew the Niobrara, ribbed with sand.
A wasting fever fed upon the Grand
And with the famishing Moreau it crawled.
All day and every day the hotwind bawled.
The still nights panted in a fever-swoon.
Dead leaves were falling in the harvest moon

And it was autumn long before the frost.
Back came the wild geese wailing for the lost—
Not there, not there! Back came the mourning
    crane.
A sunset darkened with a loveless rain;
The Northwest wakened and a blind dawn
    howled.

The winter deepened. Evil spirits prowled
And whimpered in the jungles of the cold,
Wolves of the ancient darkness that were old
Before the Morning took the Land to wife
And all the souls came loving into life
Save these alone, the haters of the warm.
Men heard them screaming by upon the storm;
And when the sharp nights glittered and were still
And any sound was big enough to fill
The world with clamor, they were gnawing fear.

The strangely wounded bodies of the dear
Grew alien. Scarce the father knew the child
So stricken, and the mother, so defiled,
By her own fire became a dreaded thing.
Wide roamed the evil spirits, ravening,
Till every village fed the Faceless Guest
With little hungers that forgot the breast
And agèd wants too long denied to care.

In vain against the formless wolves of air

The holy men wrought magic. Songs that ran
Beyond the hoarded memories of man,
With might beyond the grip of words, they sang;
But still the hidden claw and secret fang
Were mightier, and would not go away.
Grotesqueries of terror shaped in clay
To simulate the foe, and named with names
Of dreadful sound, were given to the flames;
But it was hope that perished. Empty air
Was peopled for the haunted fever-stare;
And when some final horror loosed the jaw,
What shape could image what the dying saw
That none might ever see and live to tell?

By night when sleep made thin the hollow shell
Between what is forever and what seems,
Came voices, awful in a hush of dreams,
Upon the old; and in that dreams are wise
When hearing is but silence and the eyes
Are dark with sun and moon, the weird news
          spread.
"There is no hope for us," the old men said,
"For we have sold our Mother to the lust
Of strangers, and her breast is bitter dust,
Her thousand laps are empty! She was kind
Before the white men's seeing made us blind
And greedy for the shadows they pursue.
The fed-on-shadows shall be shadows too;
Their trails shall end in darkness. We have sinned;

And all our story is a midnight wind
That moans a little longer and is still.
There was a time when every gazing hill
Was holy with the wonder that it saw,
And every valley was a place of awe,
And what the grass knew never could be told.
It was the living Spirit that we sold—
And what can help us?"

     Still the evil grew.
It fell upon the cattle, gaunt and few,
That pawed the crusted winter to the bone.
The weirdly wounded flesh of them was blown
To putrid bubbles. Diabolic fire
Burned out the vain last animal desire
In caving paunches, and their muzzles bled.
They staggered, staring. And the wolves were fed.

So Hunger throve. And many of the lean,
Who, having eyes for seeing, had not seen,
And, having ears for hearing, had not heard,
Fed hope a little with the wrathful word
And clamored 'round the agencies. "Our lands,"
They said, "we sold to you for empty hands
And empty bellies and a white man's lie!
Where is the food we bought? Our children die!
The clothing? For our people shiver. Look!
The money for the ponies that you took
Ten snows ago? The Great White Father's friends

Have stolen half the little that he sends.
The starving of our babies makes them fat.
We want to tell the Great White Father that.
We cannot live on promises and lies."

But there were weighty matters for the wise
In Washington, and bellies that were round;
And gold made music yonder, and the sound
Of mourning was a whisper.

                       So the young,
In whom wild blood was like a torrent flung
Upon a rock, grew sullen, brooding war.
What was it that the Sioux were waiting for?
To die like cattle starving in a pen?
Was it not better men should run as men
To meet the worst?

               And wrinkled warriors sighed,
Remembering the way their brothers died
Of old to make the living rich in tales.
"Go up the hills," they said, "and search the vales,
And count our battle-ponies by their breaths—
Ten thousand smokes! The grass they eat is death's,
And spirits hear the whisper of their feet.
Dream back for fighting men their bison meat;
Unlive these many winters of our sin
That makes us weak: then let the war begin,
And we will follow mighty men and tall.

Where are they?"

   And the young men thought of Gall,
The wild man-reaper of the Little Horn,
Grown tame at last, a sweater in the corn,
A talker for the white man and his way.
They thought of Red Cloud, doddering and gray,
And of the troubled twilight of his eyes,
Turned groundward now; of Spotted Tail, the wise,
Become a story seven winters old;
And, better to be sung than to be told,
The glory that was Crazy Horse. Alas!
Somewhere the heart and hand of him were grass
Upon a lonely hill!

   The winter died.
Once more, as though a wish too long denied,
Became creative in a fond belief,
The old Earth cast her ragged weeds of grief,
And listened for the well-belovèd's words,
Until her hushes filled with singing birds
And many-rivered music. Only men
Were paupers in the faith to dream again,
Rebuilding heaven with the stuff of woe.

But when the northern slopes forgot the snow
And song betrayed the secret of the nest
Too dear to keep, begotten of the West
A timid rumor wandered—vaguely heard,

[9]

As troubled sleepers hear the early bird
And lose it in the unbelieving night.
'Twas all of wrong grown weaker than the right,
Of fatness for the lowly and the lean,
And whirlwinds of the spirit sweeping clean
The prairie for the coming of the dead.
And many strove to say what someone said
That someone said, who had it from the Crows,
To whom Cheyennes or else Arapahoes
Had brought it from the Snakes. And one by one
Strange tongues had brought it from the setting sun
Across the starving lands where men endure
To live upon the locust and are poor
And rabbit-hearted. And a valley lay
Among the mountains where the end of day
Clings long, because those mountains are the last
Before the prairie that is never grassed
Rolls on forever in dissolving hills.
And in that valley where the last light spills
From peaks of vision, so the rumor ran,
There lived a man—or was he but a man?—
Who once had died, and verily had trod
The Spirit Land, and from the lips of God
He knew how all this marvel was to be.

'Twas very far away.

                    A naked tree
Awakened by the fingers of the Spring,

But lacking the believing sap to sing,
Has nothing but the winter moan to give.

The vague tale made it harder still to live
Where men must dream the right and bear the
    wrong.
And so another summer, like a song,
Sad with an unforgettable refrain—
Green promises forgotten by the Rain—
Droned to the dying cadence of the leaves.
And winter came.

          But as the wood believes
At last the evangelic winds of March,
When eagerly the bare apostate larch
Avows the faith of cedars in the sun,
And cottonwoods confess the Living One,
And scrub-oaks, feeling tall against the blue,
Grow priestly with the vision; so the Sioux
Thought better of the iterated tale.
For every westwind knew about the vale
Beneath the shining summits far away;
And southwinds hearkened what they had to say,
And northwinds listened, ceasing to deride.
The man had died, and yet he had not died,
And he had talked with God, and all the dead
Were coming with the whirlwind at their head,
And there would be new earth and heaven!
                             So

It happened, when the grass began to grow
That spring of 'eighty-nine, the dream took root
In hearts long fallow. And the fateful fruit
Greened in the corn-denying summer heat;
And dry moons mellowed it and made it sweet
Before the plum took color, or the smoke
That was the gray-green rabbit-berry broke
Along the gullies into ruddy sparks.
It seemed no secret to the meadow larks.
In clamorous and agitated flights
The crows proclaimed it. In the stifling nights,
When latent wonder made the four winds still,
The breathless watching of a starry hill
Revealed some comprehension not for speech.
And wheresoever men might gather, each
Would have some new astonishment to share.

But when the smell of frost was in the air
Of mornings, though the noons were summer yet,
The oft-shared wonder only served to whet
The hunger for a wonder real as cold
And empty bellies.

    So the wise and old
Held council. "Let us see him with our eyes
And hear him with our ears—this man who dies
And talks to God—that we may know the way;
For all our words are shadows, and the day
Is yonder, if the day be anywhere.

And who would go?"

                    Good Thunder, Kicking Bear,
Short Bull, Flat Iron would, and Yellow Breast.
So once again the man-compelling West,
Sad mother of dissolving worlds, lured on.
And when the awed adventurers were gone,
Behind them fell the curtain of the snow.

And now the moon was like an elkhorn bow
Drawn to the shaft-head, wanting but a mark;
And now a shield against the doubting dark;
And now it withered, and was lost again:
And as the moon, the phasic hope of men
Measured the winter, slow with many a lack.
For less and less the jaded news came back
From regions nearer to the setting sun—
Re-echoings of wonders said and done—
That faith might flourish briefly in the green:
And sorrow filled the silences between
With troubled voices. What if, far away,
As sunset proves but ordinary day,
The dream-pursuers only sped their dreams?

But when along the cataleptic streams
Spasmodic shudders ran; and in the lee
Of browning slopes the furred anemone,
Already awed by what might happen next,
Stood waiting; and the silences were vexed,
Between crank winds, with moaning in the sloughs—

Though still the grasses slumbered—came the news
Of those five seekers homing. Like a fire
Before a banked-up southwind of desire
Unleashed at last, it swept the tawny land.
The smoke of it was all along the Grand
When first the valley of Moreau took light
From where it bloomed in tumult on the White,
Seeding the fallows of the Big Cheyenne.
The living Christ had come to earth again!
And those who saw Him face to face, and heard,
Were bringing back the wonder of the Word
Whereby the earth and heavens would be new!

And suddenly the prairie took the hue
Of faith again. The rivers understood;
And every budding, gaunt-limbed cottonwood
Experienced the Cleansing of the Blood.
The tall clouds bent above the lowly mud.
A holy passion whitened into flame
Among the plum-brush.

                    Then the seekers came
With awe upon their faces.

II

THE COMING OF THE WORD

Was it fright,
Some prescience of the whirlwind of the light
About to break, that gripped the white men's hearts
At Pine Ridge? How the foolish dreamer starts
And strives to hold his futile world of sleep,
When lo, it is the morning, deep on deep,
That takes the world! Could agency police
Arrest the Word? And would the Wonder cease
To be the Wonder even in a jail?
Too deep for laughter, humor sped the tale
Of four returning seers behind the bars!
Was not their story written in the stars
When first the gleaming bubble of the air
Was blown amid the darkness?

Silent there
The knowers waited, patient as the stone
That has the creeping æons for its own
And cares not how the little moment drips.
The prison key had only locked the lips

Against a word already on the wing.
Two days endured the white men's questioning
Before those faces that were like the sky
When clouds have vanished and the nightwinds die
And daybreak is a marvel to the hills.
And when that silence conquered jaded wills,
The four emerged with nothing less to say.

Now Kicking Bear, sojourning on the way
To learn among the north Arapahoes
What slant of vision might illumine those,
Came burning with a story for the Sioux.
Already was the Wonder coming true
Along Wind River where the people trod
The dances taught them by the Son of God,
And there were signs and portents of the end!
The eyes that Death had emptied of the friend
Were being filled again, but not with tears.
The sudden sleep that falls among the spears
And arrows, when the dizzy sun goes black
And all the hoofs are hushed, was giving back
The healed young bodies of the sons and sires.
Dead mothers came to mend the family fires
Long fed by lonely hands; and young they were,
Each fairer for the garment folding her—
The richly beaded years!

                    And now there ran
Among the Ogalalas, man by man,

A secret whisper. And it came to pass
When early stars had found a looking glass
In White Clay Creek, and others came to stare,
The owls were startled in a valley there,
And all the kiotes hushed to hear the rills
Of people trickle inward from the hills
And merge into a murmur by the stream.

Now where the chattering campfire dimmed the
    gleam
Of stars, to build with momentary light
A wall of blindness, inward from the night
A shadow moved, took substance from the flare,
And half a man and half a ghost stood there
Searching the breathing darkness round about.
A sudden hush acclaimed him like a shout;
For in his flame-lit face, as though they heard,
Men saw the singing splendor of the Word,
Before he strove to darken into words
What only thunderstorms and mating birds
Might utter in the heyday of the sap,
When Earth with all her children in her lap
Has made her story credible again.

The hush grew big with miracle; and then
Good Thunder spoke. "My relatives," he said,
"Believe and cry no more! The dear, the dead
Are coming with a spring forever green!
Already they are marching! We have seen;

These eyes have seen the Savior! He has come!
His feet are on the prairie!"

                              Stricken dumb,
With breathless, open mouth and startled eyes,
He seemed to hear in lingering surprise
The trailing thunder and the meadow lark
Of what was uttered. From the outer dark,
As though it were the unbelieving world
That fretted yet awhile, a hoot-owl hurled
Its jeering laughter through the knowing hush.

The Word came back upon him with the rush
Of spring delayed, of rain and river-thaw
And universal burgeoning. "We saw!
With little hearts our journey was begun,
For maybe we were men who chased the sun
To find the land where always there is light;
They race with their own weakness, and the night
Outcreeps their running. So the way stretched long,
But still the right was weaker than the wrong;
Earth starved her children still; the same sky
         stared;
The people prayed and suffered; nothing cared
That there was woe wherever there were men.
And often when the day went out again,
Homesick beneath the old familiar star,
The same fear mocked us. Who by going far
Shall find the good? And who by going fast

Shall overtake it?

> But we came at last
Upon the holy valley. It was bare;
And if the summer ever had been there,
Now nothing but the gray old sagebrush knew.
Around it, higher than the eagles flew,
The shining mountains stood, and every peak
Was listening to hear the stillness speak
With tongues of thunder; but our steps were loud.

And then we saw—we saw!

> There was a crowd
That spoke strange tongues. With every wind that
> blows,
From lands where almost no one ever goes,
From countries, maybe, near to where earth ends,
Queer peoples came and mingled and were friends
With us and with our neighbors; for the wings
That bore the holy news were like the Spring's,
And nowhere had men questioned what it meant
In any tongue; but everywhere it went,
Dry hearts were greening. Is there any land
So far and strange it cannot understand
The drumming thunder and the singing rain?

And then he came—he came!

> We saw him plain;

For suddenly, across a little draw
Upon the higher bank beyond, we saw
A Piute man; and that, at first, was all.
His hair was to the ears, and he was tall,
And maybe he was thirty winters old.
His face was broad. He wore against the cold
A coat and hat and boots that white men wear.
It could have been a white man standing there,
But for his face. He carried in his hand
An eagle's wing. We could not understand,
For only with our eyes we saw him yet.
Who travels far shall see the same sun set;
Upon the longest trail the home stars rise;
And while we saw him only with our eyes
The Holy One was nothing but a man.

He smiled upon us kindly and began
To speak strange words, and they were dark like
      smoke;
But while I stood and wondered what he spoke,
There came a meaning like a spirit flame;
And then I saw the man was not the same.
He burned until his body was all light;
And if he were a brown man or a white,
I did not think at all. I only knew
How all that we had heard was coming true;
But all I knew no tongue can ever say.
Then like a shadow fell the common day,
And with my eyes I saw him as before,

A Piute man; but there was something more
That made me cry, though like a rustling tree
My body was, and like a bird in me
My heart was glad.

                    Awhile his words ran loud
And buzzed in many tongues among the crowd
Till all had heard them and the tongues were
    stilled.
Then I was feeling how his low voice filled
The world again; and it was like a light
That made me see how everything was right,
And nothing ever died or could be old.

So, bit by bit, we heard the story told
In many broken words. You too shall hear;
But feeble is the tongue and dull the ear,
And it is with the heart that you shall know.

Now all this came to pass three snows ago,
About the time when plums were getting good,
And he had gone to make his winter wood
Among the mountains. He was feeling strong.
His woman and his children went along,
And all of them were happy there together.
The air was sharp, but it was sunny weather;
The winds were still.

                    Now while the children sang
And laughed and chattered, and the axe strokes rang

Against the mountain, he could feel a change
Come over him, till everything was strange.
He listened for the noise the children made;
But all the air was empty and afraid
Of something coming. Then he tried to call
His woman; but he made no sound at all.
And while he wondered, with his axe held high,
The hollow stillness of the earth and sky
Broke down in thunder, and the mountains bowed
And flowed together, whirling like a cloud
A big wind strikes. Then everything was black.

But right away, it seemed, the world came back,
So queer and bright he knew that he had died.
The light of things was coming from inside
And cast no shade! It was like dreaming deep
And waking on the other side of sleep
To know that he had never waked before.
Still in a way that would have been a roar
In this world, all at once the pines became
The rushing up of something like white flame
That spread and hovered at the top, and then
Drooped back with many limbs and fell again
In burning showers, wonderful to see;
For all the seasons of an earthly tree
Were shortened to the blinking of an eye.
He saw the spirit forests flashing by
In generations up the mountainside;
They came and went, but nothing ever died

Nor could be old. The shapes that went and came
Were ways in which the something like a flame
Lived young forever; and the flame, he knew,
Was Wakantanka;[1] for the mountains too
Were holy with it, and the soft earth glowed,
Till it was only light that lived and flowed
To make the shapes of animal and man,
The rooted and the winged. Where one began
The other did not end, for they were one,
All coming from and going to a sun,
That drew him now. And as he rose to go,
He saw his other body there below
Burn swiftly with the holy flame and pass
Into a happy greening that was grass
Along some hill remembered from a dream.
Then he was flowing with a mighty stream
Of living light that did not make him small,
Though he was lost in it. He lived in all
The stream at once, for everything that is
Became one glowing body that was his,
And there was nothing in it near or far.
He was alive, alive in every star,
And he could feel the rivers and the rills,
The grass roots nursing on a thousand hills.

Then, all at once, some meadow of the air
Was sweet with faces blooming everywhere
About him. There were many that he knew,

[1] The Great Spirit.

[23]

But all were dear. Dim shadow-bodies grew
Beneath them, swaying with a mournful sound
And feeling for remembered shadow ground
To root in—hills of fog and valleys dim
With autumn rain, that he could feel in him
Like all the tears that men have ever shed.

But when he would have wept, behold there spread
New earth beneath; and from the glow thereof
The shadow-forms took flesh, and all above
Was living blue; and eyes have never seen
The green with which that breathing land was
    green,
The day that made the sunlight of our days
Like moonlight when the bitten moon delays
And shadows are afraid. It did not fall
From heaven, blinding; but it glowed from all
The living things together. Every blade
Of grass was holy with the light it made,
And trees breathed day and blooms were little suns.
And through that land the Ever-Living Ones
Were marching now, a host of many hosts,
So brightly living, we it is are ghosts
Who haunt these shadows feeding on tomorrows.
Like robes of starlight, their forgotten sorrows
Clung beautiful about the newly dead;
And eyes, late darkened with the tears they shed,
Were wide with sudden morning. It was spring
Forever, and all birds began to sing

Above them, marching in a cloud that glowed
With every color. All the bison lowed
Along the holy pastures, unafraid;
And horses, never to be numbered, neighed
Like thunders laughing. Down the blooming plains,
A river-thaw of tossing tails and manes,
They pranced and reared rejoicing in their might
And swiftness. In the streams of living light
The fishes leaped and glittered, marching too;
For everything that lived looked up and knew
What Spirit yonder, even in that day,
Was blooming like a sunrise.

                              And the way
Was shortened all at once, and here was there,
And all the living ones from everywhere
Were hushed with wonder. For behold! there grew
A tree whose leafage filled the living blue
With sacred singing; and so tall it 'rose,
A thousand grasses and a thousand snows
Could never raise it; but all trees together,
When warm rains come and it is growing weather
And every root and every seed believes,
Might dream of having such a world of leaves
So high in such a happiness of air.

And now, behold! a man was standing there
Beneath the tree, his body painted red,
A single eagle feather on his head,

His arms held wide. More beautiful he seemed
Than any earthly maiden ever dreamed,
In all the soft spring nights that ever were,
Might be the one of all to look on her.
He had a father's face, but when he smiled,
To see was like the waking of a child
Who feels the mother's goodness bending low.
A wound upon his side began to glow
With many colors. Memories of earth,
They seemed to be—of dying and of birth,
Of sickness and of hunger and of cold,
Of being young awhile and growing old
In sorrow. Now he wept, and in the rain
Of his bright tears the holy flower of pain
Bloomed mightily and beautiful to see
Beyond all earthly blooming, and the tree
Was filled with moaning. All the living things,
With roots and leaves, with fins or legs or wings,
Were bowed, beholding; and a sudden change
Came over them, for all that had been strange
Between them vanished. Nothing was alone,
But each one knew the other and was known,
And saw the same; for it had come to pass
The wolf and deer, the bison and the grass,
The birds and trees, the fishes in the streams,
And horse and man had lost their little dreams
And wakened all together.

                              Softly crooned

The Tree, for now the colors of the wound
Became a still white happiness that spread
And filled the world of branches overhead
With blossom and the murmuring of birds.
One life of light the peoples and the herds
Lived with the winged, the rooted and the finned.

The man was gone; but like a sacred wind
At daybreak, when the star is low and clear
And all the waking world is hushed to hear,
His spirit moved. The whisper of his word
Was thunder in the silences that heard,
And whirlwind in the quiet: "They shall see
At last, and live beneath the Blooming Tree
Forever!"

  Then so great a sunrise broke
Upon the man who died, that he awoke;
But it was when he wakened that he died.

He was no longer on the mountainside,
But home again and lying on his bed.
He looked about him, and the mourners fled,
Filling the door with chatterings and cries;
And, with a frightened stranger in her eyes,
His woman hugged their weeping little ones
And huddled in a corner.

   Dead four suns,
He 'rose and walked before her; but his face

Now shone with such a kindness, and the place
Was filled with light so beautiful, she knew
It was a holy vision shining through,
And wept with joy. And so, before she heard,
His woman was a mother to the Word,
The first of all believers to believe.

My people, O my people, do not grieve,
For soon shall break the ever-living Dawn."

Good Thunder ceased, and presently was gone,
A spectre fading in the ember light.
The breathing silence of the peopled night
Still felt the low voice flowing like a song,
The round face saddened with a people's wrong
And soft with pity; till a sudden flare
Revealed the whetted face of Kicking Bear,
The hungry gaze, the body taut and lean.

In wildernesses never to be green,
It seemed, his eager spirit dwelt apart,
Wild honey of the solitary heart,
The locust of the lonely soul, for food.
Now crying from an inner solitude
His voice arose and cut across the night:

"These eyes have seen the whirlwind of the Light!
These eyes have seen the marching of the dead!
These eyes have seen the Savior at their head,

And there shall be new earth and heaven soon!
I tell you, in the fullness of the Moon
Of Tender Grass Appearing [1] it shall be
That with the sprouting of the Holy Tree
The earth will shake and thunder. Hills will flow
As water, for a spirit wind will blow,
And all that is not real, but only seems,
And all who have not faith, shall be as dreams
Before that whirlwind waking in the spring.
Like chickens hovered by the mother's wing
The faithful shall be safe beneath the Tree,
And they shall lift their eyes and they shall see
The new earth and the ever-living Day.

My brother spoke, but there is more to say;
O there is more than any tongue can speak!
We did not find the one we went to seek,
A prophet, but a man like other men.
I tell you He is Jesus come again!
I saw the marks upon Him! It is so!
Have not the Black Robes [2] told how long ago
One came to save the people? It is He!
Did not Wasichus [3] nail Him to a tree?
Did they not torture Him until he died?
I saw the spear-wound bleeding in His side!
His lifted palms—I saw them white with scars!"

Unto the awful stillness of the stars

[1] April, 1891.   [2] Catholic priests.   [3] White men.

He gave the uttered marvel for a space,
Its latent thunder in his litten face,
The lightning of it in his burning stare.
"I saw!" he cried, "and many others there
Have said they saw it too, although the rest
Saw nothing. It was when He faced the West
And lifted up His hands to pray and said:
'Now I will show you the returning dead
And Him who leads them.' For a little while
His eyes were closed, and with a gentle smile
He moved His lips in silence. It was still,
And things turned strange; but nothing came until
His eyes were opened and He said: 'Behold!'
I looked; and yonder mighty waters rolled,
Dark waters that were filled with mournful sound
And crowded with the faces of the drowned
And drowning. And I knew the cries of birth
And death and all the sorrows of the earth
Were mingled yonder where a black wind swept
The desert of the waters; and I wept
For all of them I saw but could not save.
And suddenly beyond the farthest wave
A cloud appeared, a whirling, fearful cloud.
Its front was lightning and its rear was loud
With marching thunder. Rising very fast,
It grew, until it stood above the vast
Black flood, now whitened with the hands of prayer,
Beyond all counting, that were lifted there
For mercy. Then it seemed that all sound died,

And silences were voices that replied
To silences, so quiet was the world.
And in that sudden peace the cloud that whirled,
A dark and flaming fury in the van
Of endless cloud, was shapen to a man
With moons upon His robe of starry light.
The feet of Him were rooted in the night;
But upward, still and beautiful and far,
His face was daybreak, and the morning star
Was low upon his brow.

           A moment so
I saw, and almost knew what none may know
And linger in these shadows here to tell.
But as I gazed, a wind of burning fell
Upon that peace; and roaring from its deep,
The sunrise took the heavens at a leap,
And like a mighty wound the sky rained blood,
And from the sudden scarlet of the flood,
All white the souls of thousands who believed
Arose; but whom the eyes and ears deceived,
I saw them sinking.

           Then a singing cry
Of multitudes of voices filled the sky.
Four times I heard it singing—hey-a-hey!
And, looking up, I saw that it was day
Forever. Light no eye has ever seen
Was in the green, the spirit of all green,

That was the earth; the spirit of all blue
That was the sky. And in the midst there grew,
Most beautiful of all, the Blooming Tree.
And through that land, as far as I could see,
The dead were coming with their hands held high,
And it was they who sent the singing cry
To cheer us in this darkness of the sun.
But when I looked upon the Holy One
Who led the host, it all began to fade.

Then I was staring at the one who prayed,
And knew that it was He! That starry calm
Was on His face. In either lifted palm
A white scar gleamed; and there upon His side
The wound Wasichus gave Him when He died
Was like a scarlet flower.

                    I saw; and then
I saw a man who seemed like other men
And heard him saying: 'It is yet too soon.
Believe; and in the Grass-Appearing Moon
The change will come.'

                  My people, it is so!
The Holy One who came so long ago
Is even now upon the earth once more,
Preparing for the end. He came before
To help them, but they tortured Him and slew.
Themselves, they tell it! Are their hearts made new

These many, many grasses since He died?
I saw the wound still fresh upon His side
As when they made it! What shall fill the blind
But everlasting darkness? He was kind
As rain and grass the other time He came.
But I have seen the whirlwind and the flame;
And I have seen the greedy, faithless race
Before the waking fury of His face
Become a dream forgotten in the day;
And I have seen the old earth pass away
And all the faithful happy in the new.
He came to them; but now He comes to you!
He comes to you! And shall He be denied?
Woe to the deaf!"

             Upon a shrill note died
The upward straining voice, as though it failed
Midmost the peak of vision it assailed
Beyond the flight of words. And when he went,
A murmuring of wonder and assent
Was like a nightwind freshening, and blew
Among the darkened people; till they knew
That Yellow Breast stood waiting by the fire.

No lure of unassuagable desire
Had led him far and made his spirit lean.
Earth's tolerance was gentle in his mien;
The light of common day was in his eyes,
That seemed to look with half amused surprise

Upon a riddling world, and left it so.
There, generously bulking in the glow,
The radiating quiet of him spread,
And was a hush.

"My relatives," he said,
"You know me well, and many present knew
The boy I was, the common way I grew
To be a common man. It is the truth
There came to me no vision in my youth
That I might have the power to behold
The hidden things; and neither am I old
Enough in years to make me very wise.
The good and evil seeing of my eyes
I have believed; and what my ears have heard,
If it might be a straight or crookèd word,
I have considered, often being wrong.
And such a man it was you sent along
With these my brothers here, to see and say
If truly yonder at the end of day
A tale of many wonders might be so.

A man who trails an elk or buffalo
May camp with hunger or may sit to eat;
There will be meat or there will not be meat;
He shall be full or empty at the last.
But who shall trail a story? Not so fast
The blizzard flies; and like the whirling snows,
The shapes of it keep changing as it goes.

The bison is no bison, but a deer,
Or else a wolf; and it is never here,
But always it is yonder. Over there
It is an elk that changes into air.
The hunger and the hunted are the same;
And whosoever feeds upon that game,
He shall be very lean.

      And so I said
About this tale of the returning dead
And new earth coming: 'It is far away;
And big; and getting bigger every day.
So are the people's hunger and their sorrow.
The empty belly and the fat tomorrow
Have made a story.'

     But I did not speak.
I went along to see. My heart was weak;
And often as I went I wept alone
To think how big the hunger would have grown
When we came back with nothing.

       We are here
And you have heard already. If the ear
Alone had told me half of what I know,
I must have wondered if I heard it so,
Or how good men turned foolish on the way.
But I myself have seen; and I will say
No more than I have seen. I must believe
For what I saw; and if my eyes deceive,

How can I know that I know anything?
The coming of the grasses in the spring—
Is it not strange so wonderful a tale
Is really true? Did mornings ever fail,
Or sleeping Earth forget the time to grow?
How do the generations come and go?
They are, and are not. I am half afraid
To think of what strange wonders all is made!
And shall I doubt another if I see?

No vision in the heavens came to me.
I saw the mountains yonder gleaming tall,
And clouds that burned with evening. That was all.
But while the Holy One was praying there,
I felt a strangeness growing in the air
As when, a boy, I wakened in the night,
And there was something! Faces queerly bright
Were there about me, lifted to the skies;
And I could see some wonder filled their eyes,
Though mine were dark and many others too.

I might believe that everything is true
The Holy One has said and you have heard.
There was a living power in His word
I never felt before; for when He spoke,
It seemed that something lifted like a smoke
And common things were wonderful and new.
But still I could not tell you it is true,
Had I not seen.

This happened on the way
When we were coming home and stopped to pray
Among the Blue Clouds [1] yonder, and to rest.
Of all our neighbors farthest to the west,
They were the first to hear, and first to learn
The dance He said would make the dead return
And new earth blossom. They were dancing then;
And many died and came to life again
Refreshed and very happy; for they said
That they had seen their dear ones who were dead
And visited with them. I longed to see;
I danced, I prayed. But nothing came to me
Until the evening of the seventh day.
They made a feast before we came away,
And it was at the lodge of Sitting Bull, [2]
The holy man. The moon was rising full.
A melting wind had died in pleasant weather,
And we were twenty sitting there together
Around the fire. Two places in the ring
Were empty. Sitting Bull began to sing
A sacred song. Four times he sang, and then
He made a prayer that he might see again
His father and his mother, and that we
Who sat to eat with him might also see
The dearest of our dead.

A queerness came

[1] Arapahoes.
[2] Sitting Bull, the Arapahoe.

[37]

On everything. I could not hear the flame
That chattered in the wood a while before.
A little whisper would have been a roar,
It was so still. Then suddenly it seemed—
And if I dreamed, the twenty of us dreamed
The same dream all together—something grew
Like moon-fog where the places for the two
Had been left empty. Growing from the ground,
It shaped itself and thickened, while a sound
Of voices far away came singing through;
And there were faces, many that I knew,
About the fog—a cloud of shining faces.

And then I saw there were no empty places!
A woman and a man were sitting there,
With wrinkled cheeks, at first, and snowy hair,
And with a weary question in their eyes.

But all at once—and there was no surprise
Till afterward—I saw that they were young,
And seemed to know the robes of light that clung
About them were the winters they had known
Together here, all beautifully sewn
With colored sorrows. I could smell the breath
Of green things on the other side of death—
It seemed a kind of singing. Bison herds
Sang with them, weaving voices with the birds,
The horses and the women and the men—
One happy tribe rejoicing. And again

Still as a place of death, the world grew still;
And all around, the night began to fill
With people, people. Eagerly they pressed
About us, happy-faced; and with the rest
My father came, as much alive as I!

Twelve snows ago, it was, I saw him die
That blizzard day we fought beside the Tongue [1]
While with the starving horses and the young
The starving women fled. It was a dim
And fearful battle, and I clung to him,
For something of the boy was in me yet.
We had no powder left. With clubs we met
And struck at shapes that loomed and danced away
And roared and blazed about us in the gray
Half-night of snow. I heard my father scream
Beside me there; and often in a dream
I've heard him since, to waken in a chill
Of terror; for the boy was in me still,
Though I was tall. Face downward in the snow
I saw him flounder like a buffalo,
Lung-shot. I stooped to help. He tried to shout
Some word; but only black blood bubbled out.
Then I went killing crazy. Shadows fell
Or fled about me; and I cannot tell
How long it was till nothing but the storm
Was whirling 'round me, and I knew the warm
Wet weight I staggered under."

[1] The fight with Miles on Tongue River, January, 1877.

[39]

Yellow Breast
Fell brooding, while that battle in the West
Woke in the women memories of woe
That wailed across the dark.

                              "Twelve snows ago,"
He said at length, "I watched my father's face
Bleed empty, and a stranger in his place
Come staring. And I wept and prayed to die.
But now he came, as much alive as I—
O more alive than I have ever been!
His body glowing by a light within,
He came to me and smiled. Upon my head
He laid his hand. 'Believe, my son!' he said;
'Believe, my son!'

                              And whether late or soon,
I do not know; but all at once the moon
Was shining as before. The fire was low,
And twenty sitting in the ember glow
Were staring at each other in dismay;
For all had seen what verily I say
I saw. And I believe it."

                              Yellow Breast
Was gone, and voices of the dark confessed,
Sweeping the gamut in their reach for awe,
The bright faith shared, until the people saw
The face of Short Bull eager in the gleam.

It was no dreamer's wistful with the dream.
Surely, he dwelt familiarly at ease
Amidst a world where divers certainties
Took root to flower and flourish in a green
Congeniality. The ready mien,
The bustling manner and the bright, shrewd eyes,
Too certain of their seeing to be wise,
Proclaimed the man.

                "My relatives!" he cried;
And, waiting while the distant echo died,
His face went grave with what he meant to say.
"This thing must be set going right away,
And I will tell you all that you must do.
What you have heard is true; but more is true,
And you shall hear and know it for the truth.
I did not doubt this story. From my youth
There had been voices. I was very young
When first the Spirit taught me in the tongue
Of birds. And often in some quiet place
The dead have spoken to me, face to face,
And dreams have shown me things that were to be.
I say this story was not strange to me,
Because I dreamed it just before it came
By living tongues. The Savior is the same
I saw in sleep. I knew it would be so.
His very words I knew. Hear now and know
What wonders He can make.

One day we sat
To hear Him teach. He wore a broad black hat,
A common hat that any man could wear;
But what He did with it before us there
Not any man could do. He held it, thus,
Before Him, with the hollow turned to us,
And closed His eyes and prayed a little while
In whispers. Then He smiled a happy smile
And passed His eagle feather 'round the brim
And said, 'Behold!'

                I looked into a dim
Deep hollow that was growing; and it grew
Until it was so deep and wide, I knew
That nothing was beyond it, or could be.
And as I wondered at it, I could see
The stars were coming out. They came and came
Until their shining made a soft white flame
That left no empty places in the night.
Then I could see that it was getting light
With dawn that seemed to come from everywhere,
As much like singing and as much like prayer
As seeing. Then the very world was day;
And when I think of it I cannot say
If I was in it, for it seemed inside,
Like being very glad. But it was wide
As I could feel, and there it did not cease.
It went forever in the blue, blue peace
That was the sky; and in the midst there glowed

A green, green world where singing rivers flowed
And leaped and glittered with rejoicing fish;
And deer and elk and bison had their wish
On blooming hills; and happy valleys fed
The singing tribes of men; for none was dead
That ever lived.

       All this I saw, and then
I saw the hollow of the hat again
And it was empty. Truly, some who sat
With us that day saw nothing but a hat,
Because they did not have this gift of mine.
Black Kiote saw, and so did Porcupine,
Almost the same as I; and others too.

There is no end to all that He can do,
This Son of Wakantanka. Beasts and birds,
They say, come close and talk to Him in words,
The same as other people. Trees and grass,
They say, get greener when they feel Him pass,
The way they freshen in a sudden shower.

There is one other story of His Power
That I will tell. Before we came away,
The Savior told us, 'If you stop and pray
When you are very weary, I shall know,
And something good will happen.' It was so.
There was a prairie, dead with thirst, and wide
Beyond a hundred looks. On every side

We stared, and there was nothing anywhere;
And we were weary. So we made the prayer
And slept, believing something would befall.
When we awoke we weren't there at all,
But far upon our journey! This is true.

There is a sacred dance He sent to you
And it will make you see the world of light
And all your dear ones yonder. Every night
The people all shall dance with sacred song,
The little children also. All night long
The fourth night, they shall dance until the day;
Then they shall bathe and all go home to pray
Until the time for dancing comes again!
The Savior, He has said it! Woe to men
Who hear not! I have spoken. Hetchetu!"

He ceased, and as he went the people knew
The eager, whetted voice of Kicking Bear
That from the starry wilderness of air
Shrilled in the hush: "Believe! Be not afraid!
Believe! Believe! And safe within its shade
The Holy Tree will fold you on that day
When all the ancient stars shall blow away
Like autumn leaves, and solid hills shall flow
Like water! Woe to men who hear not! Woe
To faithless men, the blind who will not see!
The Savior, He has said it! Even He,
The Savior said it!"

On a distant hill
The wild voice faltered briefly; and the still
Expectant hollow of the night seemed dense
With dwellers in a breathless imminence
Of whirlwind wonder straining to begin.
A breath might break the world-wall, bubble-thin,
Between this starry seeming and the Light.

The brush-fed embers filled the startled night
With sudden darkness. Presently there came
A shadow moving inward to the flame;
And it was Red Cloud standing in the glow.
Deep voices and the women's tremolo
Acclaimed him still a mighty man and wise,
Despite the wintered hair; the rheumy eyes;
The groundward gaze, incuriously dim;
The once compelling upward thrust of him,
In shrinking shoulder-droop and sagging girth
Now yielding slowly to the woman Earth
The man that was—half woman at the last.
But when at length he raised his face and cast
That unexpecting gaze about him there,
The dignity of stoical despair
Revealed the hero yet.

His voice was low,
Less seeming to be sent than made to grow,
By some indwelling power of the word,
Among the crowd:

"My people, you have heard;
And it is good. The winter and the spring,
The blooming summer and the withering,
The generations and the day and night
Are only moving shadows; but the Light
Is Wakantanka. When our young feet pass
Across the holy mystery of grass,
Our eyes are darkened for the ways we go;
And that is good. We see, and it is so;
We hear, and know it; touch, and it is true.
For to be young is to believe and do,
As rooted things must blossom and be green.
But when the eyes grow weary, having seen,
And flesh begins remembering the ground.
There is a silence wiser than all sound,
There is a seeing clearer than the sun;
And nothing we have tried to do, or done,
Is what the Spirit meant.

                The Earth is old;
Her veins are thin, her heart is getting cold;
Her children mumble at her empty paps;
The bison, crowding in her thousand laps,
Have turned to spirit. And the time is near.

This word is good that we have come to hear.
This word is very good."

                With gray head bowed,

He stood awhile in silence, and the crowd
Was still as he.
                  At length he stole away,
A shadow unto shadows.

III

THE DANCE

Every day
No Water's Camp was growing near the mouth
Of White Clay Creek, lean-flowing in the drouth.
What matter if the doomed, unfriendly sky,
The loveless grudging Earth, so soon to die,
Ignored the supplication of the lean?
Rains of the spirit, wonders in the green,
Bloom of the heart and thunders of the Truth,
Waking the deathless meadow lark of youth,
Were yonder. So the village grew. And most
Who came there felt the leading of the ghost;
But if the clever in their own regard,
Amused contenders that the hills were hard
And could not flow, came mockingly to see,
They saw indeed.

They saw the Holy Tree,
A sapling cottonwood with branches lopped,
Set in the center of a ring, and topped
With withered leaves. Around it and around,

Weaving a maze of dust and mournful sound,
The women and the children and the men
Joined hands and shuffled, ever and again
Rounding a weird monotony of song,
Winged with the wail of immemorial wrong,
And burdened with the ancient hope at prayer.
And now and then one turned a knowing stare
Upon the empty dazzle of the skies,
Muttering names, and then, as one who dies,
Slumped to the dust and shivered and was still.
And more and more were seized upon, until
The ring was small of those who could not see;
And weeping there beneath the withered tree,
They sang and prayed.

           But when the sleepers woke
To stagger from the dust, the words they spoke,
As in a dream, were beautiful and strange.
And many a scoffer felt a still swift change
Come over things late darkened with the light
Of common day; as in a moony night
The rapt sleepwalker lives and is aware,
Past telling, in the landscape everywhere
About him till no alien thing can be,
And every blade of grass and weed and tree,
Seed-loving soil and unbegetting stone,
Glow with the patient secret they have known
These troubled whiles, and even men shall know.

One moment, shrewdly smiling at a show,
The clever ones could see a common pole,
The antic grandmas, little children, droll
With grownup airs, the clowning men who wept,
And dust. But suddenly, as though they slept
And dreamed till then, to wake at last and see,
Swift saps of meaning quickened to a tree
The rootless bole, the earth-forgotten thing
With starveling leafage; and the birds would sing
Forever in that shielding holiness.
A joy that only weeping can express
This side of dying, swept them like a rain
Illumining with lightning that is pain
The life-begetting darkness that is sorrow.

So there would be more dancers on the morrow
To swell the camp.

         The Moon When Ponies Shed [1]
Had aged and died; and, risen from the dead,
The Moon of Fatness,[2] only in the name,
Haunted the desert heavens and became
A mockery of plenty at the full,
Remembering the thunders of the bull,
The lowing of the countless fatted cows,
Where now it saw the ghostly myriads browse
Along a thousand valleys, still and sere.
But mightily the spirit of the year,

[1] May.   [2] June.

At flood, poured out upon the needy ones
The Light that has the dazzle of the sun's
For shadow, till the very blind could see.

And then it was beneath the withered tree
Young Black Elk stood and sent a voice and wept;
And little had he danced until he slept
The sleep of vision; for a power lay
Upon him from a child, and men could say
Strange things about his seeing that were true,
And of the dying made to live anew
By virtue of the power. When he fell
The sun was high. When he awoke to tell
The silent crowd that pressed about the place
Of what he saw, with awe upon its face
The full moon rose and faltered, listening.

It was, he said, like riding in a swing,
Afraid of falling; for the swing rose high;
And faster, deeper into empty sky
It mounted, till the clutching hands let go,
And, like an arrow leaping from a bow,
He clove the empty spaces, swift and prone.
Alone he seemed, and terribly alone,
For there was nothing anywhere to heed
The helpless, headlong terror of the speed,
Until a single eagle feather blew
Before him in that emptiness and grew
Into a spotted eagle, leading on
With screaming cries.

                    The terror now was gone.
He seemed to float; but looking far below,
He saw strange lands and rivers come and go
In silence yonder. Far ahead appeared
A mighty mountain. Once again he feared,
For it was clothed in smoke and fanged with flame
And voiced with many thunders. On it came
And passed beneath. Then stretching everywhere
Below him, vivid in the glowing air,
A young earth blossomed with eternal spring;
And in the midst thereof a sacred ring
Of peoples throve in brotherly content;
And he could see the good Red Road that went
Across it, south to north; the hard Black Road
From east to west, where bearers of the load
Of earthly troubles wander blind and lost.
But in the center where the two roads crossed,
The roads men call the evil and the good,
The place was holy with the Tree that stood
Earth-rooted yonder. Nourished by the four
Great Powers that are one, he saw it soar
And be the blooming life of all that lives,
The Holy Spirit that the good grass gives
To animals, and animals to men,
And they give back unto the grass again;
But nothing dies.

                    On every drying rack,
The meat was plenty. Hunters coming back

Sang on the hills, the laden ponies too.

Now he descended where the great Tree grew
And there a man was standing in the shade;
A man all perfect, and the light He made
Was like a rainbow 'round Him, spreading wide
Until the living things on every side,
Above Him and below, took fire and burned
One holy flame.

   "Then suddenly He turned
Full face upon me and I tried to see,"
Young Black Elk said, "what people His might be;
But there was cloud, and in the cloud appeared
So many stranger faces that I feared,
Until His face came smiling like a dawn.
And then between two blinks the man was gone;
But 'round the Tree there, standing in a ring,
Twelve women and twelve men began to sing:
'Behold! the people's future shall be such!'
I saw their garments and I wondered much
What these might mean, for they were strangely
  wrought.
And even as I thought, they heard my thought
And sang reply: 'The people clad as we
Shall fear no evil thing; for they shall see
As you have seen it. Hundreds shall be flame.'

Then I was blinded with a glow that came

Upon them, and they vanished in bright air
And wordless singing.

                  Standing lonely there,
I thought about my father who is dead
And longed to find him. But a great Voice said,
'Go back and tell; for there is yet more wrong
And sorrow!'

            Then a swift wind came along
And lifted me; and once again I knew
The fearful empty speed. Face down I flew
And saw a rushing river full of foam,
And crowds of people trying to get home
Across it; but they could not; and I wept
To hear their wailing. Still the great wind kept
Beneath me. And you see that I am here."

Young Black Elk ceased; and, thinking of the dear
Good days of plenty now become a tale,
A woman, old and withered, raised a wail
Of bitter mourning: "It was even so
The way the young man saw it. Long ago
I can remember it was just the same,
The time before the bad Wasichus came,
That greedy people! All good things are dead,
And now I want to die." Her sorrow spread
Among the women like a song of pain,
As when the ponies, heavy with the slain,

[54]

Return from battle and the widows crowd
About them, and the mothers.

                              When the shroud
Of moony silence fell upon their woe,
Young Black Elk spoke again: "What shall be so
Forever, I have seen. I did not sleep;
I only woke and saw it. Do not weep;
For it is only being blind that hurts.
Tomorrow you shall make these holy shirts
For us to wear the way I saw them worn.
Clothed in the Holy Spirit, none shall mourn
Or come to harm along the fearful road."

So on the morrow happy women sewed
In all the tepees, singing as they made
Of odds and ends and empty sacks of trade,
The rags and tatters of their earthly need,
Unearthly raiment, richly wrought indeed
For all the love they stitched in every hem.
And good old men of power painted them
With sacred meaning: blue upon the breast,
A moon of promise leading to the west,
The end of days; and, blue upon the back,
A morning star to glimmer on the black
And fearful road; the neck and fringes red,
The hue of life. An eagle feather sped
On either arm the homing of the soul.
And mighty with the meaning of the whole,

The work was finished.

                 Death became afraid
Before the dancing people so arrayed
In vision of the deathless. Hundreds burned
With holiness.

              But when the cherries turned
From red to black, while Summer slowly died
And in her waiting hushes prophesied
The locust, and the lark forgot his song,
There fell the shadow of the coming wrong
And yet more sorrow that were left to bear.

The Agent came to see; and he was there
With all his world about him. It was sure
And solid, being builded to endure
With granite guess and rumor of the eyes,
Convincingly cemented with surmise
Against all winds of fancy and of fraud.
The height of it was high; the breadth was broad;
The length was long; and, whether bought or sold,
The worths thereof were weighable in gold,
His one concession to the mysteries.
As common as the growing of its trees,
And natural as having wakened there
Quite obviously living and aware,
His world was known.

So clearly they were mad,
These dancing heathen, ludicrously clad
For superstitious doings in a day
Of Christian light and progress! Who could say
What devilment they hatched against the whites,
What lonely roofs would flare across the nights
To mark a path of murder!

It must cease.

Surrounded by the Indian police,
Who sat their mounts importantly, half proud
And half abashed to wear before the crowd
Of relatives the master's coat of blue,
He spoke: "This thing is foolish that you do,
And you must stop it!" Still as though a trance
Had fallen on the interrupted dance,
The people listened while a half-breed hurled
The feeble thunder of a dying world
Among them: "It is bad and you must stop!
Go home and work! This will not raise a crop
To feed you!"

Yet awhile the silence held,
The tension snapping with a voice that yelled
Some word of fury; and a hubbub broke.

As when across the dust and battle-smoke
The warrior hails the warrior—"Hokahey!

Have courage, brother! Let us die today!"—
The young men clamored, running for their guns.
And swarming back about the hated ones,
They faltered, waiting for the first to kill.
Then momently again the place went still,
But for the clicking locks. And someone cried:
"Your people tortured Jesus till He died!
You killed our bison and you stole our land!
Go back or we will kill you where you stand!
This dance is our religion! Go and bring
Your soldiers, if you will. Not anything
Can hurt us now. And if they want to die,
Go bring them to us!"

                    Followed by the cry,
As by a stinging whip, the Agent went.

That night one mourned: "It was not what you
      meant!"
Alone upon a hill he prayed and wept;
"Not so you taught me when my body slept.
Great Spirit, give them eyes, for they are lost!"

IV

THE SOLDIERS

When plums were mellowing with early frost
And summer was a ghost, with noons that made
The ponies droop in any thinning shade;
With nights that in a hush of tingling air
Still listened for the geese; to Kicking Bear
There came an eager word from Sitting Bull
Up yonder on the Grand: "The winds are full
Of stories. Are they echoes of a lie?
If truly, as we hear, your dancers die
And visit with the dead and then return
Alive and well, my people want to learn.
Come up and teach them."

                       Singing of the day
That was to be, the prophet rode away;
But not alone if what some say be true,
That when he loomed against the shining blue
Upon the final hilltop, strangely large,
The sky was filled with horsemen at the charge
That whirled about him going. Then the sky
And hill were empty.

                    Dreaming days crept by,
And nights were glinting bubbles on the strain,
Blown vast with silence. Then at last the crane
Came crying high; a roaring norther sped
The startled geese, and panic voices fled
Above the sunless and the starless land.
Now came the news of dancing on the Grand
With many tales of wonder-working there;
And of the ghostly might of Kicking Bear
A story lived on every tongue and grew.
It told how, riding northward, rumor flew
Before him, till the Agent heard and feared
At Standing Rock. So when the prophet neared
The home of Sitting Bull, a jingling band
Of Metal Breasts [1] made dust across the land
And trotted up to seize him.

                    Unafraid
He waited. Then it seemed that something made
A solid wall about him, thin as light;
For suddenly the horses reared in fright
And shied away before him, shivering.
There came a queerness over everything
That made the horses and the riders seem
As though they gazed on terror in a dream,
And could not stir. "My brothers, foolish ones,"
He said, "what have you put into your guns
To kill the Spirit? I am Kicking Bear,

    [1] Indian police, so named for their metal badges.

                    [60]

But I am not alone. Behold! the air
Is crowded with my warriors! Look and see!"

He raised an eagle feather. Silently
A little while he prayed; and as he prayed
The horses lifted up their heads and neighed,
Beholding; with a catching of the breath,
Wide-mouthed upon the Other Side of Death
The riders gazed with startled happy eyes,
Like sleepers who have wakened in surprise
To some great joy. A moment so, and then
The horses drooped, the faces of the men
Were empty; for the darkness that is birth,
The sleep that men call waking on the earth
Came back upon them. Hardly could they keep
Their saddles for the heaviness like sleep
That fell upon them as they rode away.

Thus mighty was the living Word, they say;
And mightily it flourished on the Grand.

Again a waiting stillness seized the land;
For now the snowless wind blew out and died.
Perhaps the geese had falsely prophesied
And men would never see another snow.
The listening hills and valleys seemed to know,
In that untimely warmth and straining peace,
One bird, believing, almost might release
Immortal springtime. Whisperless with awe,

What vision was it every bare tree saw?
What made the humblest weed-stalk seem aware?
The stillness of the starlight was a prayer,
The dawn a preparation, for the bird.

But in that lull of miracle deferred
Before the Moon of Falling Leaves ¹ was dark,
Who listened for the deathless meadow lark
Heard tidings of the trouble yet to be.
The singing people heard on Wounded Knee,
And terror silenced them. On Cut Meat Creek
The dancing Brulès heard, and hearts grew weak,
Lost in the swift return of common day.
The vision fled from hundreds on the Clay,
And eyes of little light went blind again.
For everywhere the feet of marching men
Were rumored. Yonder from the iron road
To south, to west, to northward, load on load,
The soldiers and the horses spawned and spread!
Where were the whirlwind armies of the Dead?
The skies were deaf. Far-journeying, the suns
Knew nothing of the Ever-Living Ones,
The shining, good, green Country of the Young.
Fear called the changing tune of many a tongue
Late lyric with the crowd: "We told you so!
Now let us see you make the hard hills flow,
And tell your Christ to hurry! He is late!"
Youths, burning for the rendezvous with Fate,

¹ November.

Were loud for battle. "Let us fight and die!"
They clamored. "Better men than you and I
Have died before us! Crazy Horse is dead!
And will it not be good to go," they said,
"Wherever he went? Living, we are poor!
How rich the dead must be! Let hills endure,
And cowards live forever if they can!"

Remembering, the ancient sorrow ran
Among the women wailing.

                              "Even so,"
The old men mourned, "we youngsters long ago
Would die to make a tale. The world is old;
Now all good stories have been lived and told,
And who shall hear them in a few more snows?"

But still the voices of the faithful rose,
Scarce heeded: "We have seen what we have seen!
Not when the world is singing in the green
The Savior comes; but when the leaf is sere
And nothing sings. Already He is near!
The Happy Ones are crowding all the air,
Beholding us! Be strong of heart to bear
This one more sorrow that must come to pass.
The Black Road ends!"

                              But withered hearts were grass,
Rich fallow for the seeding of the spark,

And, raging through the horror-painted dark
Of its begetting, panic was a flame.

To Red Leaf's camp the fleeing terrors came
On Wounded Knee, to pause and huddle there,
Fused in a hush of communal despair—
An empty ear for any voice to fill.
And thither, from some lonely vision-hill,
The vessel of an evangelic voice,
Came Short Bull, crying: "Hear me and rejoice!"

A mockery of echoes fled and failed
Among the bluffs. Some little hunger wailed,
Until a crooning mother hushed again
The ancient question only dreams of men
Have ever answered—with how many whys!

The sudden center of a thousand eyes
Made quick with hope or lusterless with care
Or quizzically narrowed, silent there
He filled the silence. For the people saw
A face it seemed some other-worldly awe
Had touched with glory. What ecstatic death
Of self in vision yielded him the breath
Of universal living for a while,
That so upon this trouble he could smile,
With such a look upon this darkness beam?
Or had the weed of self in some vain dream
Grown mightily, till everything was small

Save him, and in the glory of it all
He towered now?

                Again the shrill voice went
Among the people: "Wakantanka sent
A vision to me on the hill last night
When I was praying. Stillness and a light
Became the world; but what they said to me
Would shake these hills down, if a word could be
To say it. I will tell you what I may.
These troublesome Wasichus, what are they
To run from? Hardly to be called a race,
The color of their death in every face,
Their strength is like a shadow's. Very soon
They shall be nothing. Until now, the Moon
Of Tender Grass Appearing, it was said,
Would see the whirlwind coming of the Dead,
And hear the sprouting-thunder of the Tree.
But by a power the Spirit gave to me,
Because of trouble these Wasichus make
I will not wait until the grasses wake,
Nor shall there fall a single flake of snow,
Before I tell the Tree to sprout and grow;
The Dead to come; these solid hills to run
Like angry water; stars and moon and sun
To be as withered leaves and blow away.
And everything shall hear me and obey,
For Wakantanka said it. I have seen
Among the badlands where the earth is lean

[65]

And hardly can the cactus live for need,
The place where even now the holy seed
Lies thirsting in the dust till it shall know
My word of power. Yonder we must go
To sing and pray until the time is right
For me to speak. If soldiers come to fight,
Is not the very power in their guns
The same that lives in grasses and that runs
In winds and rivers and the blood of man,
And birds fly with it? Since the world began,
Of one great Spirit everything is made
And lives and moves. So do not be afraid.
Their guns will not go off. And when I speak,
The hearts of all their horses shall be weak,
Their knees become as water under them.
Then, beautiful with thunder, shall the stem
Burst from the shattered earth, and soar and spread
All green and singing, singing! It is said!
The Spirit said it. Hear it and rejoice!"

Astonished silence swallowed up the voice,
And for a timeless moment no one stirred,
While yet the many, fused by what they heard,
Were like a sleeper. Murmuring eddies broke
Among them, spreading as the one awoke
Into the many, mingled and were loud,
With scorn and wonder clashing in the crowd,
Belief and doubt.—'If only all believed!—
If only fools so easily deceived

[66]

Were wiser!—If the deaf would only hear!—
Could big talk fill the belly through the ear?
'Twere better to surrender and to eat!—
To fatten on Wasichu lies for meat!
There never was a better day to die!—
Lo, even now the crowding of the sky!
Behold! Believe! It could not now be long!—
The soldiers! They were coming! They were
　　strong,
Not shadows; and the babies would be killed!
The badlands! To the badlands!' Women shrilled
Above the wrangling babble and the shout
Of faith unshaken: 'There the Tree would sprout,
The shielding Tree! They could not murder souls!'

The din died in a clattering of poles,
The sound of stricken lodges coming down,
Where, petulantly buzzing 'round the town,
The women now, as one, were bent on flight
From danger. Children crying in the night
Were those to her, the woman who survives
All man's believings; whom he never wives
For all his wooing, being newly born
Forever in her passion, half a scorn,
But all a shielding fury at the test.

As with a single will the rabble pressed
To northward down the valley of the stream.
For now the driving fear, the leading dream,

The burning of the wild hearts of the young
For deeds and dyings worthy to be sung,
Became one impulse in the straggling ranks.
Far flung, the young men raged along the flanks
And rear; and lonely places were aghast
By night with flaring ranch roofs, where they
        passed,
Those harriers of cattle and of men,
For whom now briefly had returned again
The very eld of story and of song.
And steadily the rag-and-tatter throng
Grew with the sullen stragglers driven in
To share whatever fate the rest might win,
Whatever hope might feed upon despair.

Beyond the White they fled, along the bare
Unearthly valleys, awed by some intense
Divinity of knowing reticence
About them in the lunar peaks and crags,
Where wearily the questing echo lags
Behind some haunting secret that eludes
To fill the hushes of their solitudes
With sleeping thunder. Yonder, wheeling slow,
Aloofly patient, did the buzzard know
The secret? Were the jeering crows aware?

So great a void, and yet a little prayer
Could fill it and a little question drain!

The trail led steeply to a living plain
Aloft amid the life-forgetting waste,
A lonely island staring stony-faced
Upon the slow encroachment of a sea
Whereof the fluid is eternity,
And time the passing tempest, and the roar
Devouring silence. Still there, as of yore
When Earth was young beneath the primal blue,
Spring keeps with her the ancient rendezvous,
And little needs that run and root and nest
Know in the giving sweetness of her breast
The pity that is water. Grass was good
In plenty there, and stunted growths of wood
Clung to the gulches.

              There they camped to wait
The coming of the good or evil fate
That might befall them. Verily it seemed
To many that their woes were only dreamed,
And this the verge of waking to a deep
Serenity beyond the pain of sleep
Forevermore. But many, scanning far
That desolation of a manless star,
Saw, picture-written in the stuff of sense,
The affirmation of their impotence
And slow despair.

           Through breathless nights of frost
The old moon shrank, delaying, and was lost;

And wonder-weather made the brief days weird.
At last the Moon of Popping Trees [1] appeared,
A ghost above the sunset, leading on
Where all days perish in a deathless dawn,
And still no snow had fallen in the land.
Then Kicking Bear came riding from the Grand,
With words of power: 'Let the people hear
And have strong hearts! The time was very near
When Sitting Bull would come; and then, behold!
The whirlwind of the miracle foretold
Would sweep the world!'

[1] December.

V

SITTING BULL

Daylong the holy dance
Beside the Grand had murmured in a trance
Of timeless weather. Now, the stars were sharp,
And, tense with frost, the night was like a harp
For any little sound. The young moon sank.
Among the trees along the river bank
The tepees gloomed. Across the open flat
To northward, where a group of cabins sat
Beneath the hills, a window with a lamp
Revealed the one place waking in the camp,
The home of Sitting Bull.

The room was dim
With smoke, for there were nine who sat with him
And passed the pipe, in silence for the most,
As though some felt eleventh were a ghost
That moved among them. Tales of long ago
Had failed the mark, as from a sodden bow
Unfleshed the bravest arrows falter spent;
And stories that were made for merriment
Had fallen short of laughter.

Now at last
They only sat and listened to the vast
Night silence, heavy with a feel of doom.
The old wife, dreaming in the corner gloom,
Turned with a moaning like a broken song;
And, questioning a universe made wrong,
Far off by fits arose a kiote's cry
That left a deepened silence for reply—
The all-embracing answer.

Catch-the-Bear
Got up, the startled creaking of his chair,
The shuffle of his feet upon the floor
Loud in the stillness. Striding to the door,
He flung it wide and filled it, listening.
The sharp air entered like a preying thing,
The living body of the hush that prowled
The hollow world. A camp dog woke and howled
Misgiving, and the kennelled hills replied.
The panic clamor trailed away and died;
And there was nothing moving anywhere.

He closed the door, returning to his chair,
And brooded with a troubled face. "My friend,"
He said at length, "I fear how this may end.
I am afraid to see the break of day.
It might be better to be far away,
If they should come. You said that you would go.
What keeps you waiting here?"

                                    "I do not know,"
Said Sitting Bull, and gazed upon the wall
With eyes that saw not anything at all
But lonely distance that is not of space.
Without the wonted shrewdness in his face,
The lurking wit, it seemed a stranger's stare
He turned upon his friend. "I hardly care,"
He said; "I may be only getting old;
Or maybe what a meadow lark foretold
Is near me; yet I do not feel afraid.

It happened that my circus horse had strayed
One day last summer. So I went to see
A little valley where he likes to be;
But it was empty, even of the crows,
Except for something any still place knows
But sound can never tell it. That was there.
It filled the valley and it filled the air;
It crowded all about me, very still.
I stood there looking at a little hill
That came alive with something that it knew,
And looked at me surprised. The stillness grew.
Then suddenly there came a human cry
From yonder: 'Sitting Bull, your time is nigh!
Your own will kill you!'

                            It was loud and clear;
So loud I wondered that I did not hear
An echo. Yet I thought, 'Perhaps a man

Is hiding over there'; and so I ran
To see who said it, maybe out of fun,
Or maybe spite. There wasn't anyone.
But while I wondered had there been a sound
Or had I dreamed, there fluttered from the ground
A meadow lark, and with it rose again
The same cry uttered with the tongue of men,
'Your own will kill you!' Then above my head
Four times it circled rapidly, and fled.

How long I stood there thinking on the hill
I do not know; but, by and by, a shrill
Long neigh aroused me. Looking 'round, I saw
My old gray horse come trotting from a draw
And down the valley. Then the common day
Came back about me."

     Gazing far away,
He brooded. When he spoke again he seemed
As one but half awake. "Last night I dreamed
Of mighty waters, flowing swift and deep
And dark; and on that river of my sleep
I floated in a very frail canoe.
The more I longed to stop, the greater grew
The speed, more terrible for lack of sound.
I thought of help, and when I looked around,
Behold, there floated past on either side
A happy land that flourished in a wide
Blue morning; yet I did not see the sun.

Old camps I had forgotten, one by one,
Came there abreast of me and hurried by.
And someone who was happy, yet was I,
Played 'round his mother's tepee. She was young,
And nothing ever could be said or sung
To tell about the goodness of the place,
And how it was that something in her face
Could make a day so big and blue and clear.
They did not look at me; they could not hear
The cry I sent, though all the stream ahead
Was filled with mocking voices.

                           Faster sped
The river. Nothing ended or began;
And yet I saw the boy become a man,
And all about him in the whirling change
Were faces falling in and growing strange
Beneath a sudden wintering of hair;
And they were gone, and other faces there
Were round and happy in the Spring they cast,
An eye-blink long; for now the stream was fast
As wind in anger. All the days and nights
That I have lived, the hunts, the feasts, the fights,
Were there again, and being there, were gone,
So swift they were. And still my life came on.
But now the sky was not so blue and wide;
The land was not so green. On either side,
The fury of the wind of days had done
What made me weep. I could not see the sun;

[75]

But surely now it sickened to a moon,
And in the ghost of day it made were strewn
The bones of all the buffalo that were.
The Earth, our mother, had the face of her
Who sees her children's children bury theirs,
And, weary of remembering her cares,
Begins the long forgetting.

              There was night
Before me, and a fog of dying light
Behind me, and that ghost of day around;
And under me, too deep for any sound,
The mystery of water and the speed.
Then even sorrow left me in my need,
And fear, the last of friends to flee away.
I drifted into waking, and the day
Was young about me.

             It may happen so.
But still I feel the swift, dark water flow;
I feel it carry me, and do not care."

He scanned that distance with an empty stare
That slowly filled and, brimming with a smile,
Ran over into chuckles for awhile;
And then he said: "What matter? It was good!
Why mourn the young flame laughing in the wood
With tears upon the ashes? I could laugh
All night remembering, forgetting half

The happy times before the world was old.
Do you remember, friends—?"

                            And now he told
The story of the fool who, feeling wise,
Would catch a bear, and how that enterprise
Too greatly prospered. Taking either part
With highly circumstantial mimic art
And droll sobriety, as one at ease
With Truth, the chiefest of her devotees,
He built the old tale toweringly tall;
And when at last it toppled to its fall,
And ended with the strangest of all rides,
The men with streaming eyes and aching sides
Defied the vast night silence with a roar
Of laughter, till the woman on the floor
Sat up and scolded. Ever and again
The mirth, subdued, broke out among the ten,
As seeing how the panic people ran
The day the stridden bear brought back the man,
Precariously clinging by its hair,
And shouting wildly: "I have caught a bear!
Behold!"

          But when the final chuckle died,
As though that prowler in the hush outside
Came creeping in, they sat there listening,
Wide-mouthed, alert. There wasn't anything.
They heard their hearts.

"Yes, truly it was good,"
Said Sitting Bull at length; "but if I could,
I would not live it over from the first.
The goodness of the water is in thirst,
And I have drunk. That day I broke the pipe,
Two moons ago, this heart of mine was ripe
For death already. Shall the ripe grow green?
Beyond a winter's telling I have seen
Enough to make a liar choose the true,
Of wonders these Wasichus dream and do
In crowded lands beyond the rising sun.[1]
I look and see the evil they have done.
My eyes are weary. What is looking worth?

Have I not seen the only mother, Earth,
Full-breasted with the mercy of her Springs,
Rejoicing in her multitude of wings
And clinging roots and legs that leaped and ran?
And whether winged or rooted, beast or man,
We all of us were little ones at nurse.
And I have seen her stricken with a curse
Of fools, who build their lodges up so high
They lose their mother, and the father sky
Is hidden in the darkness that they build;
And with their trader's babble they have killed
The ancient voices that could make them wise.
Their mightiest in trickery and lies
Are chiefs among them. It shall come to pass

[1] He had travelled in Europe with a circus.

[78]

When these at last have stolen all the grass
And all the wood, the water and the meat,
And there is more to burn and drink and eat
Than all could use in many moons of feast,
The starving people shall become a beast,
Denied the very grasses of the chief.
But dreaming each to be the bigger thief
They toil and swarm, not knowing how their sweat
Shall turn to blood upon them. Who forget
Their mother, are forgotten at the last.
Already I have seen it in the past
Of spirit vision. It is even so.
These eyes need not to see it.

Long ago
It happened I was all alone one day
Among the mountains, where the still ones say
In silence what can make men wise to hear.
And while I listened only with the ear,
The pines were giants weeping all around.
Then suddenly there wasn't any sound,
And I could feel that I was not alone.
There was an eagle sitting on a stone
Far up, and all the air was like a crowd
That waits and listens. Then a voice was loud:
'Behold! Hereafter he shall rule the land!'

I thought and thought; I could not understand.
But I have lived to see it; for behold

The image of the eagle on the gold
These mad Wasichus worship and obey!

The worshippers shall come to be the prey!

You bid me go; but which way lives the Good?
I know my friend would tell me, if he could,
Where greens that land, the weary trail to go,
How many sleeps, and where the grasses grow
The deepest, and the waterholes are sweet.
Then would I ride my horses off their feet
To find that country! But the Spirit keeps
The secret yet awhile.

                                How many sleeps?
One sleep, the last and deepest of them all!
I will not ride, my friends."

                                Beyond the wall
He gazed again, brows lifted, eyes a-shine,
While louder grew the breathing of the nine
Who watched him. What unutterable day,
Death-deep in night, a heavy sleep away,
Had found the lonely summit of his hope?

They saw the shadow of his waking grope
Across his face.

                        He turned to them and said:

"They who have seen this vision of the dead
Have seen what they have seen; and it is good.
But foolish hearts that have not understood,
They make a story out of it that lies.
The blind ones! They would have it with their
        eyes!
The deaf ones! They would hear it!

                                        Even so,
Almost my heart persuaded me to go.
So big it was with hate and ripe to die,
That it would set men fighting for a lie—
And what to fight with, starving as they are?"

He 'rose. "I wonder if the daybreak star
Is up," he said; "the night is getting old."

Out in the starry glitter of the cold
They followed him and, muffled in their breaths,
Stood shivering, and gazed.

                                The hush was death's
The East was blind. Knee-deep along the flat,
A fog came crawling. Nothing moved but that.

"My friends," he said at length, "it might be best
To go to bed and get a little rest
Before the morning. It is well with me."

They gripped his hand in silence. Silently,
Like spirits wading in no earthly bog,

They went, and vanished in the deeper fog
Along the river.

        Still he waited there,
His ghostly breath ascending like a prayer,
The peace of starlight falling for reply
Upon his face uplifted to the sky,
And 'round his body, like a wraith of doom,
The ground-fog rising.

            Presently the gloom,
Where stood the rail corral, gave forth a neigh
That screamed across the night and died away
Into a coaxing nicker. With a start,
The cold, quick clutching of a panic heart,
He turned. There, etched upon a patch of stars,
The old horse thrust his head across the bars,
Ears pricked to question what the master meant.
A warming glow about his heart, he went
And stroked the steaming muzzle that was pressed
With happy little sounds against his breast,
And begging whimpers. Thus remembering,
Again he saw the dazzle of the ring
And heard the heaped-up thunders of applause,
The roaring like a wind that swept in flaws
The hills of men.

       How far it was away!

He threw the old gray horse a feed of hay,

And slapped his neck; then, hunching to the cold,
Went off to bed.

            The slumber of the old
Fell heavy on the night. The stars burned dim.
The East wore thinner.

               Something startled him.
A moment, 'risen from a dreamless deep,
He floated on the surface of his sleep
And knew the fog had found an open door.
It seemed to make a sound along the floor
Of stealthy feet that whispered!

              "Who is there?"
He said. A blue spurt sputtered to a flare
Of yellow. Was the lark's word coming true?
With badges glinting on their coats of blue
And rifles in their hands, the room was full
Of cold-eyed kinsmen!

            "Hurry, Sitting Bull!"
Said one; "Get up and dress!"

             The match flare died.
From over yonder by the riverside
A long cry 'rose. The dogs began to bark.
And in the moment's nightmare of the dark
Where startled voices clashed, the woman screamed.

A new flare sputtered, and the lamplight gleamed
Upon a witch's face and fury there,
Eyes burning through the tangle of her hair,
Mad with the wrath of terror for the dear.
"Begone!" she raged. "What are you doing here?
You dogs! You jealous woman-hearted men,
I know you! Go, and let us sleep again!
You, Bullhead there! What have we done to you?
Red Tomahawk, for shame! for shame! I knew
Your father, and a man! He lies at rest
And does not see that metal on your breast,
That coward's coat! I do not want to see!
Begone, Dakotas that you ought to be!
Fat dogs you are, that bad Wasichus keep
To sneak and scare old people in their sleep,
And maybe kill them! Ee-yah! Get you hence!"

Stone to the torrent of her impotence,
They crowded 'round the man upon the bed
And strove to dress him. "Hurry up!" they said,
"The White Hair¹ wants you!"

                              Placid in their clutch,
He answered: "Friends, you honor me too much!
Am I a warrior going forth to die
That you should dress me? Yet no child am I
That cannot dress himself. Be patient, friends!
If somewhere hereabouts the long trail ends,

¹ McLaughlin, Agent at Standing Rock Reservation.

I would not reach it naked. Let me dress!"

He stood now, jostled in the eager press
Of men who clamored, angrily afraid,
"Be quick! Be quick!" For all the doubtful aid
Of tangled hands that fumbled, tugged and tore,
And shoved him on, he reached the open door
Not garmentless.

The sounding world seemed black.
But when the vision of the dark came back,
The star-concealing mist, a chill blind gray
With some diluting seepage of the day,
Was full of moving shapes. And there were yells,
The jingling merriment of little bells
About the necks of ponies milling 'round,
And more hoofs rumbling on the frozen ground
Out yonder.

Forth into the dying night,
With Bullhead on his left, and on the right
Red Tomahawk, they crowded him along,
While from the doorway followed, like a song
Of rage that rises on a wing of woe,
The old wife's wailing: "Whither do you go?
There is a name that you have carried far,
My man! Have you forgotten who you are
That cowards come and drag you out of bed?
It would be well if Sitting Bull were dead

[85]

And lying in his blood! It would be well!
But now what story will be good to tell
In other winters?"

         Desperate alarm
Tightened the fingers clutching either arm;
And in his leaping heart that meadow lark
Sang wildly.

        Now against the fading dark
There loomed a bulk he knew for Catch-the-Bear,
And yonder was the old horse waiting there
Already saddled. For a ghost to ride?

He struggled in a net of arms, and cried:
"Hopo-o-o-o Hiyupo! Cola,[1] come ahead!
Come on, I will not go!"

         The great voice fled
Among the people, leaving in its path
An inward surging and a roar of wrath.
Then from the bulk of Catch-the-Bear there broke
The crash and ruddy bloom of powder smoke,
And Bullhead tumbled to a backward sprawl;
But in the very eyeblink of the fall,
His rifle muzzle flared against the back
Of Sitting Bull. A moment hanging slack
Amid a sag of arms, the limp form fell.

[1] Friend.

A swift hush ended in a howling hell
Of madmen swarming to a bloody work,
And horses screaming in the flame-smeared murk
That hid the slow dawn's apathetic stare.

Now while men fought and died about him there,
The circus horse remembered. Once again
That rainless storm upon the hills of men,
The barking of the guns about the ring,
The plunging of the horses, and the sting
Of powder smoke! He knew it well! He knew
The time had come to do what he could do
The way the master wished it.

                              With the proud
Old arching of the neck, he kneeled and bowed;
Then, having waited overlong in vain
To feel the lifting hand upon the rein,
He 'rose and, squatting on his haunches, sat
With ears alert; for always after that
It thundered.

                    Lo now, even as of old
The hills applauded and their thunders rolled
Across the ring! But now they crashed and blazed
About him strangely. Haughtily he raised
A hoof, saluting, as a horse should do,
Though fearfully the storm of voices blew—
Hoarse-throated panic shrilling into yells

Of terror at the bursting of the shells
From where broad daylight lay upon the hill
Alive with soldiers.

                There he waited still
When all his people, save the weary ones
Who slumbered in the silence of the guns,
Had run away, and strangers crowded 'round.
Impatiently he pawed the bloody ground
And nickered for the master.

              People say
It happened in the badlands far away
That certain of the faithful 'rose to see
The morning star. In tense expectancy
They huddled, watching, on a weird frontier
Of sleep and waking wonder, hushed to hear
What meaning labored in the breathless vast
Of silence. Would that morning be the last
Of earthly mornings? Would the old sun rise?
Or did they feel the day that never dies
Preparing 'round them?

              Like the leaden ache
Of some old sorrow, dawn began to break
Beneath the failing star. And then—*he came!*

Gigantic in a mist of moony flame,
He fled across the farther summits there,

That desolation of an old despair
Illumined all about him as he went.
And then, collapsing, like a runner spent,
Upon the world-rim yonder, he was gone.

'Roused in the shiver of the common dawn,
The buzzing village marvelled. 'Lo! the dead
Were drawing near!' "A warning!" others said;
"Some very evil thing will happen soon!"

VI

THE WAY

Now in the bleak fulfillment of the moon
The ragged hundreds of Sitanka's band,
With many who had fought upon the Grand,
Were fleeing southward from the big Cheyenne.
Behind them were the haunts of faithless men,
The feeble-hearted and the worldly wise,
And all the little deaths of compromise
That are the barren living of the blind.
What if the world they strove to leave behind
Still clung a heavy burden on the old,
And starving children shivered in the cold,
And plodding mothers, with the bitter-sweet
Remainder of their aching hearts to eat,
Mourned for the wailing hungers at the breast?
A little farther on there would be rest
Forevermore, there would be warmth and food.

But now the northwind found their solitude
And, like the wolfish spirit of the world
They fled from, all day long it howled and swirled

About their going, loath to let them go,
Too bitter for the pity of the snow
That soothes and covers and is peace at last.

Nightlong about their tepees raved the blast.
The moonset and the morning came as one.
Cold as the sinking moon, a triple sun
Arose to mock them. Day was like a chain
Of little linked eternities of pain
They lengthened step by step. And all day long
With feeble voices tortured into song
They raised again the ancient litany
With freezing tears for answer: "Pity me!
Have pity on me, Father! All is lost!"

Hunched to the driving needles of the frost,
With tucked-in tails and ready for the crow,
The ponies, now one flesh at last in woe
With man, the master, swelled the feeble wail.
They heard the wolves of chaos in the gale,
And nothing heeded, but the pain that cried,
The cry of pain.

       The frail flesh, crucified,
Forgot the Spirit. Truth was in the storm,
And everlasting. Only to be warm,
Only to eat a little and to rest,
Only to reach that Haven of the Blest
Amid the badlands! Were not Kicking Bear

And all his faithful people waiting there
With fire and shelter, food and friendly eyes?
The sick hope built an Earthly Paradise,
A stronghold set against the hounding fear
Of iron-footed furies in the rear,
For surely there the soldiers could not come.

Once more night howled the moon down. Drifting
    dumb
Before the wind on fire with flying rime,
The aching center of a ring of Time
That was the vast horizon glittering,
All day they searched the south. No living thing
Moved yonder. What had happened to the band
Of young men riding to the Promised Land
For succor? Was it days or years ago?

Hope conjured ponies toiling in a row
Across the prairie rim with heavy packs,
And hunger matched the plenty on their backs
With their delay. But, empty with despair,
The frost-bleared eyes beheld the empty air,
The empty earth.

        An irony of flame,
The blown-out day flared whitely when they came
At last to where the prairie, dropping sheer,
With slowly yielding battlements of fear
Confronts the badlands. Long forgotten rain

Had carved a stairway to the lower plain,
And there beside a clump of stunted plum
They pitched their tepees.

Purple dusk went numb
With icy silence as the great wind froze
Above the wall and ceased. And the moon 'rose
With nibbled rim, already growing old,
To flood with visibility of cold
The aching stillness. Moaning hungers slept.

But they who woke with dumb despair or wept
Beside the tepee fires they kept alight,
Heard in the moon's mid-climbing of the night
The sound of hoofs approaching and a shout
That set the ponies neighing. Tumbling out,
The village swarmed about the little band,
Their skin-rack horses staggering to a stand
With frosted muzzles drooping to the ground.
There were no packs.

Men searched without a sound
Those moonlit faces, ghostly to the eyes
That looking on no Earthly Paradise
Had left so hollow and no longer young.
"We saw," one said, dismounting, with a tongue
That stumbled as the feet that sought the warm,
"We saw their ashes blowing in the storm.
They have surrendered. They were starving too.
We saw their ashes."

              Shrill the mourning grew
Among the women for the hope that failed,
And in the tepees children woke and wailed
In terror at the mystery of woe.

But now a brush-heap crackled to a glow
Midmost the village, and a leaping flame
Darkened the moonlight. There Sitanka came
And lifted up a broken voice and cried:
"Be still and hear!"

              The sound of mourning died,
And in a catch of hope the people turned,
Searching the father face of him that yearned
Upon them like a mother's; but his tears
Could not unman it. Bowed with more than years,
His body swayed with feebleness and shook
As with a chill, and ashen in his look
Devouring fever smouldered. When he spoke,
It seemed the slow words strangled with a smoke
Of inner fire beneath the clutching hand
Upon his chest.

              "Be strong to understand,
My children. Keep the faith a little yet.
The Earth forgets us; shall we then forget
The Spirit and that nothing else is true?
The Savior's wound grows beautiful in you!
Lift up your hearts made holy with the spear!

This is the way. The time is very near,
For now we have so little left to lose.
But for this failing flesh that we must use
A little longer, butcher ponies. Eat,
And thank the Spirit not alone for meat.
Choose not between the evil and the good.
Give thanks for everything!"

                   Awhile he stood
With hands upraised. The whispering fire was loud,
So deep the silence of the gazing crowd,
For surely he grew taller by a span
And some deep well of glory over-ran
The tortured face.

              "Great Spirit, give us eyes,"
He prayed, "to see how sorrow can be wise,
And pain a sacred teaching that is kind,
Until the blind shall look upon the blind
And see one face; until their wounds shall ache
One holy wound, and all the many wake
One Being, older than all pain and prayer."

A little longer he stood weeping there,
That morning in his look. Then, old and bent
With suffering, he tottered as he went.
But still the people listened for a space,
As though the meaning of that litten face
Groped in the silence for the ears of men.

[95]

Then cold and hunger, mightier again
Than spirit, came upon them with a rush
And not to be denied.

                    They gathered brush
And kindled morning, lyric with the lark
Of pain and terror in the outer dark
Where ponies screamed and strangled to the knife.

Alone amid some borderland of life,
Sitanka, in a drowse of fever, dreamed—
Or did he wake? For suddenly it seemed
The stars were icy sweat; the heavens swooned
With anguish of a universal wound
That bled a ghastly gloaming on the night;
And, thronging in that agony of light,
The faces, faces of the living things
That strive with fins or roots or legs or wings,
Were all alike. "It was the Savior cried!"
He gasped. But one there patient at his side
Crooned to her man and stroked his fevered head.
"It was the ponies. Go to sleep," she said.
"But there was one," he muttered, "only one."

Until the low moon faded for the sun,
Gray specters of a prairie *aeons* dead,
Haunting the silence with a word unsaid,
The butte tops glimmered with the festal light,
And heard against the reticence of night

The flesh-fed spirit dare again to sing
Of day, wherein no more the famishing
Would feed upon the famished, pain on pain.

The still dawn came relenting. Not in vain
Now seemd the night's renewal of the hope.
The bright air stung, but every sunward slope
That joined their singing as the people passed
Recalled the ancient yearning to be grassed,
Dreaming of April and the world made new.
Serenely the immense, believing Blue
Awaited, cleansed of cloud and void of wings,
The resurrection of the myriad Springs,
The miracle of thunder-soaring boughs.

Above Sitanka, in a burning drowse
Upon his pony-drag, men leaned to hear;
For in the broken babble of the seer
Were tidings of the Ever-Living Dead,
And mightily their meaning grew and spread
Among the band.

                              Before the whet of night
They camped and killed more ponies by the White
And kindled fires and feasted. Sleep came soon.

A crimson dawn burned out the bitten moon.
The Sun came walking with a face benign.
Now up the valley of the Porcupine

They labored, eager with a growing sense
Of some omnipotent Benevolence
Mysteriously busy in the warm
Still air. The naked hills forgot the storm.
The beggared plum-brush, rooted in the lees
Of winter, listened for the bumblebees
And almost heard them.

                      Growing with the sun,
A southwind met the people on the run
And clamored 'round them like a happy throng.

The flanking bluffs gave back their flights of song,
Applauding with the boom of ghostly drums,
Wind-beaten: "Lo! Behold! The Whirlwind
    comes,
And they shall know each other as they are!—
Upon my forehead shines the daybreak star.
I show it to my children. They shall know!—
A nation marching with the buffalo,
Our dear ones come! The tender grass is stirred!
The tree grows taller, greening for the bird!
A sacred wind is walking with the day!"

Now while they paused to rest beside the way,
Sitanka, rousing from a stupor, cried
A bitter cry. And surely, then, he died:
For when the people crowded 'round him there,
Bleak with the frozen horror of a stare

An alien face appalled them.

                              And the wail
Of women shrilled above the moaning gale,
Lamenting for the well-belovèd one;
And men, with nothing to be said or done,
Stood waiting, waiting, unashamed to weep.

The nightward shadow lengthened from a steep
Above them, and the chill of evening ran
Along the wind. The women now began
To make the dear one ready for the grass.

And then it was the wonder came to pass!
He drew a moaning breath. A tremor shook
His limbs. The empty winter of his look
Began to fill. There broke upon his face
From some immeasurably distant place
A growing light. Awhile he lay, a spent
Wayfarer, studying in wonderment
That cloud of frightened faces 'round about,
As though the very miracle of doubt
Amazed him. "Children, children, I have seen!"
He panted; and the shining of his mien
Made morning in the overhanging cloud
Of huddled faces. "Did I cry aloud?
And did you fear for me, and did you weep?
It was a dream that came to me in sleep.

It seemed that we were camped about a hill
With many soldiers; and the place was still
And full of fear. Then from the hillside broke
A whirling storm of powder flame and smoke,
And all the valley in its roaring path
Screamed back for pity to the hill of wrath
That flashed and thundered in the bloody rain.
Then all the voices were a spear of pain,
A great white spear that burned into my side,
And with a voice that filled the world I cried,
'Have pity on us all, for we are blind!'

There came a speaking stillness, very kind.
The whole land listened, and began to green.
Upon the flat and up a long ravine
The heaped and scattered dead began to 'rise,
And faces, glad and shining with surprise,
Were turned on shining faces, brown and white;
And laughing children, with their wounds of light,
Went running to the soldier-men to play,
For those were uncles who had been away
And now were happy to be back again;
And twice I looked to see that they were men,
So very beautiful they were and dear.
And when I thought the Savior must be near
And looked to see Him walking, white and tall,
Across the prairie, there was light; and all
The grasses in the world began to sing,
And every queer and creeping little thing,

That loves the grass, was singing, having shed
Its load of strangeness; and the singing said:
'Behold, behold, behold them! It is He!

Then such a rain of knowing fell on me,
I bloomed all over.

         It is getting dim;
But still I see we feared and hated Him,
My children. In this blindness of the sun
Are many shadows, but the Light is one;
And even if the soldiers come to kill
The Spirit says that we must love them still,
For they are brothers. Pray to understand.
Not ours alone shall be the Spirit Land.
In every heart shall bloom the Shielding Tree,
And none shall see the Savior till he see
The stranger's face and know it for his own.
This is the secret that the grass has known
Forever, and the Springs have tried to say."

The voice became like singing far away,
And ceased. The people listened yet awhile,
For still it lingered in the loving smile
That faded slowly into quiet sleep.

They heard the wailing wind upon the steep,
Remembering the loneliness of grief.
And eyes of wonder, searching for belief,

Beheld a shining that was not the sun's
In eyes that saw, despite the darkened ones
Of those who tapped their foreheads, being shrewd.

A holy stillness filled the solitude
That night; and tenderly the stars bent low
To share with men the faith that grasses know
And trees are patient with it. All the bare
Hushed hilltops listened and became aware
How nothing in the whole world was afraid.
And when the moon came, withered and delayed,
Like some old woman wedded to the crutch,
She seemed as one who, having mothered much,
Must mother yet wherever there is sorrow.

There woke yet more believers on the morrow
That lacked but bloom and verdure to be May.
And so they made a new song on the way.
Of joy they made it. "Father, I have seen
The stranger's face! Behold, my heart is green!
The stranger's face made beautiful to see!"

Amid the silence like a spirit tree,
Wide-branching, many rooted, soared the tune.

VII

WOUNDED KNEE

Now in the waning of the afternoon
They neared the place where, topping the divide,
A lonely butte [1] can see on every side
Where creeks begin and where they wander to.
And lo! the guidons and the crawling blue
Of cavalry approaching down a hill!

The people halted, staring, and were still
With wonder. Was the vision growing real?
They heard the leather singing with the steel.
The long hoof-murmur deepened. Summits rang
With happy echoes when a bugle sang.
The sleek-necked horses knew their kin and neighed
A joyous greeting. Up the cavalcade
The trailing welcome clamored to the end;
And, rousing to the music of the friend,
The feeble ponies nickered back to those.

Then mightily the people's song arose,
And all the valley was a holy place

[1] Porcupine Butte.

To hear it: "Father, I have seen his face,
The stranger's face made beautiful! Behold,
My sprouting heart is green!" Around them rolled
The steel-shod thunder, closing in the rear.
"The stranger's face made beautiful and dear,"
They sang with lifted hands, "I see! I see!"

Along a flat beside the Wounded Knee
They camped at sundown, lacking neither wood
Nor water; and the tattered tepees stood
Within the circled tents beneath a low
And sloping hill where, glooming in a row,
The wagon-guns [1] kept watch upon the town.

A gentle spirit with the night came down,
And like a father was the Soldier Chief.
Strong-hearted, of the plenty of his beef,
The plenty of his bread, he gave to eat;
And plenty was the sugar to make sweet
His many-kettled coffee, good to smell.
And much he did to make the children well
Of coughing, and to give the mothers rest;
And for the burning in Sitanka's breast
His holy man made medicine that night.

One people in a blooming ring of light
They feasted; and within the blooming ring
A song was born: "For every living thing

[1] Cannon.

We send a voice! Lean closer, One Who Gives!
A praying voice for everything that lives!
Lean close to hear!"

Sleep came without a care.
Above them, with a face of old despair,
The late moon brooded, watching for the sun.

Almost it seemed the miracle was done
That morning of a weather-breeding day.
The spell of bright tranquility that lay
Upon the land wrought eerily with sound,
And strangely clear the voices were around
The crackling fires, yet dreamily remote.
Straight-stemmed, the many smokes arose to float
Dissolving umbels in the hollow blue,
Where, measuring some endless now it knew,
A patient, solitary buzzard wheeled.
Northwestward where the Black Hills lay concealed
Behind the bluest ridge, a faint cloud 'rose,
As though the peaks and flowing slopes of those
Were stretching up to see what might betide.

And now Sitanka, when a bugle cried,
Awakened to the prison of his bed.
A nearer neighbor to the shining dead
Than to the darkly living ones, he lay
And heard, as in a dream and far away,
A deep hoof-rumble running in the land

And briefly singing voices of command,
Clipped upward with an edge to be obeyed.
Again the bugle cried and, ceasing, laid
A sudden stillness over all the camp.

A troop-horse pawed no longer, ceased to champ
The bit and shake the bridle. Awful grew
That stillness of the vision coming true,
That crystal moment of eternity
Complete without a shadow. He could see,
As though his tepee were illumined air,
The whole enchanted picture breathing there
About him: all his ragged band between
The horsemen, southward, skirting the ravine,
And footmen, northward, ranged beneath the hill;
The soldiers on the summit, tall and still
Beside those war-dogs crouched on eager paws
With thunder straining in their iron maws
The leash of peace; the children unafraid,
With thirsting eyes and mouths agape to aid
In drinking all that splendor, gleaming brass
On serried blue!

                    He listened for the grass.

Scarce real in seeming as the hush it broke,
A voice arose. The Soldier Chieftain spoke.
Remotely clear, the sound itself was kind,
And, trailing it a little way behind,
A voice made meaning that was gentle too.

The speaking ceased. Among the tepees grew
A busy murmur like the buzz and boom
Of bumblebees at work on cherry bloom
In hollows hushed and happy in the sun.

Now surely was the miracle begun,
And all the little strangers without name,
No longer strange, made ready to proclaim
The secret all the Springs have tried to say;
And grasses, greening for the deathless day,
Took breath before the world-renewing song!

And then, as though the dying world of wrong
Cried out before the end, Sitanka heard
The high haranguing voice of Yellow Bird
Above the lulling murmur: "Foolish ones
And blind! Why are you giving up your guns
To these Wasichus, who are hardly men
And shall be shadows? Are you cowards, then,
With hearts of water? Are you fools to heed
A sick man's dreaming? Stab them, and they bleed
No blood of brothers! Look at them and see
The takers of the good that used to be,
The killers of the Savior! Do not fear,
The Nations of the Dead are crowding here
To help us! Shall we shame them? *Do as I!*"

Beneath that final spear-thrust of a cry
The very silence seemed to bleed and ache.

Now!—now!—if but a single seed should wake
And know its Mother, or a grass-root stir,
The sap of pity in the breast of her
Must flood the world with Spring forevermore!

A gun-shot ripped the hush. The panic roar
Outfled the clamor of the hills and died.

And then—as though the whole world, crucified
Upon the heaped Golgotha of its years,
For all its lonely silences of tears,
Its countless hates and hurts and terrors, found
A last composite voice—a hell of sound
Assailed the brooding heavens. Once again
The wild wind-roaring of the rage of men,
The blent staccato thunders of the dream,
The long-drawn, unresolving nightmare scream
Of women and of children over all!
Now—now at last—the peace of love would fall,
And in a sudden stillness, very kind
The blind would look astonished on the blind
To lose their little dreams of fear and wrath!

A plunging fury hurtled from its path
Sitanka's tepee. In a gasp of time
He saw—like some infernal pantomime
A freeze of horror rendered motionless
Forever—horses rearing in a press
Of faces tortured into soundless yells,

Amid the gloaming of the Hotchkiss shells
That blossomed in a horizontal flaw
Of bloody rain that fell not.

                              Then he saw
One face above him and a gun-butt raised;
A soldier's face with haggard eyes that blazed,
A wry wound of a mouth agape to shout,
And nothing but the silence coming out—
An agony of silence. For a span,
Unmeasured as the tragedy of man,
Brief as the weapon's poising and the stroke,
It burned upon him; and a white light broke
About it, even as a cry came through
That stabbed the world with pity. And he knew
The shining face, unutterably dear!
All tenderness, it hovered, bending near,
Half man, half woman, beautiful with scars
And eyes of sorrow, very old—like stars
That seek the dawn. He strove to rise in vain,
To say "My brother!"

                              And the shattered brain
Went out.

              Around the writhing body still,
Beneath the flaming thunders of the hill,
That fury heaped the dying and the dead.
And where the women and the children fled

Along the gully winding to the sky
The roaring followed, till the long, thin cry
Above it ceased.

              The bugles blared retreat.
Triumphant in the blindness of defeat,
The iron-footed squadrons marched away.

And darkness fell upon the face of day.

The mounting blizzard broke. All night it swept
The bloody field of victory that kept
The secret of the Everlasting Word.